D1374136

THE
Ultimate
No 4 No

TAMIKA NEWHOUSE

AUTHOR OF *KISSES DON'T LIE*

The Ultimate No-No 4 by Tamika Newhouse

Delphine Publications focuses on bringing a reality check to the genre urban literature.
All stories are a work of fiction from the authors and are not meant to depict, portray, or represent any particular person.

Names, characters, places, and incidents are either the product of the author's imagination or are used fictitiously, and any resemblances to an actual person living or dead are entirely coincidental.

The Ultimate No-No 4
© 2013 Tamika Newhouse

ISBN 13 - 978-0989090643

Cover Design: Odd Ball Designs
Layout: Write On Promotions
Editor: Tee Marshall
Published by Delphine Publications
www.DelphinePublications.com

Printed in the United States of America

Dedication

I watch your drive to be successful and it always motivates me to do more. For David.

Acknowledgements

Here I am on my ninth book. I started off as a teen mom with a dream. I started off as a girl with this bottled up ambition. My journey to this point was not an easy one. I have loved and lost, fought and won, cried and cheered, but mainly I have tried to stay focus on what my purpose in life is.

It's not many who I can say contributed to my growth. Nicola thank you for always being that listening ear and for being the number one chick in my life. Marckus thank you for being my best friend through everything. Kayla thank you for being my oldest friend, you get me and I get you I love you.

Thank you to my Delphine Publications family for being my extended love ones and trusting your career in my hands. Special shout out to Christina S. Brown for always ensuring I have the best media, Carol Mackey for giving Delphine Publications a platform, Selena James for believing in me early on, Davida and Candice for providing a great image for Delphine.

Lastly thank you to my readers for always supporting my works. I travel to over twenty cities per year and you always come out to support me. You have no idea how your very existence in my life gives me so much power. Thank you so much.

I am already writing on book ten so I have to make this short. I will see you all at the end of this book. Welcome to my mind...

Message to my readers

So the final installment to The Ultimate No-No is here. Make sure you have read the previous books to understand this entire story. In order read

The Ultimate No-No

The Ultimate Moment No Regrets

Will Love Ever Know Me

Kisses Don't Lie

Kisses Don't Lie 2

All of these titles connect to this final book here. I hope that you have enjoyed these characters. You will see a lot of them in books to come. Such as Denim will have his own book soon, you heard that here first. But as far as Nitrah, Charmaine, Dahlia, and Jazz all good things must come to a end.

Welcome to my mind, enjoy this read and if you enjoyed definitely tell a friend.

Muah

Tamika

PS: Feel free to tweet me or instagram your questions twitter @TamikaNewhouse and instagram @BossladyTamika

The Ultimate No-No 4

By

Tamika Newhouse

The year 2000 before the SCAM

I was so uncomfortable I did not know what to do. I tugged at my shirt to pull it down over my belly button, but despite my efforts that did not work. I could not wait till this was over with. I did not want to be up here anyway.

I was pushed from behind as someone whispered, "Nitrah pay attention you are up next." I turned around to eyeball my sister, Tierra. I rolled my eyes and stuck out my tongue.

Tierra was the reason I was standing on the side of the stage at Soul Bounce, a local poetry spot, preparing to recite some of my poetry. I had never performed anything of mine before and right now I still didn't want to do it.

Turning around, I looked across the stage and my eyes landed on Denim. He winked and gave me a head nod. I blushed, trying to stay focused.

Tierra hit me from behind again and said, "Stop paying attention to Denim's nappy headed ass and focus. You're not going to embarrass me tonight."

Rolling my eyes, I said "Shut up. I am going to rock this." I tried to convince myself with that line.

The announcer finally came up and said, "Now coming to the stage is Nitrah Hill. She is a sophomore at the

University of Texas and this is her first time performing tonight. So y'all give her a warm welcome to the Soul Bounce stage."

The crowd went into a routine applause. I knew they weren't excited about having fresh meat on stage. I lowered my head and took the first step onto the stage. My knees where shaking beneath me. I turned to see Tierra give me a reassuring nod.

Denim had dropped out of school and was now the house DJ at the club. He began playing my favorite Lauryn Hill jam knowing that it would ease my mood.

I took the microphone in my hand and said, "Thank you soul sista for the welcome and thank you Soul Bounce for allowing me to be here. I won't hold you long because as they said I am new to this. But I am going to take my time and speak from my heart if you don't mind."

The crowd applauded and rooted me on. I stood in the middle of the floor and clinched the microphone and closed my eyes. My mouth was moving even before I knew it.

They say love is blind.

Shit I guess that's why I didn't see.

I was supposed to be able to know when I was being lied to.

Supposed to know when the man I loved was playing me.

Blind. Shit maybe I was deaf too.

Because the lies he told sounded like the truth.

They spoke of everything I wanted to hear.

Baby I love you, I'll never hurt you, oh that's just a friend.

True, I played a part in this game.

This little game we play called "Catch the Heartbreak."

It requires two players.

One calling the shots and the other following along.

Imagine which player I was.

Blind and deaf. Shit this ain't even the half of it.

With my mind belonging to him and my soul connected to his, I was destined to be blind.

Blind to a liar. A man who swore I was his number one.

Maybe I was his number one, but not his only one.

Maybe I wasn't worthy enough to be spoken the truth to my face.

Maybe, just maybe I was only worth the lies.

I think back and wonder. Wonder if it all was a lie?

Was I recruited to play this game? This game we call love. Or was I traded in for a new player?

This game.

You can't play it blind and deaf.

My eyes closed jumped open with the eruption of applause. My eyes now bulging out of my head as I scanned the room. There were so many people clapping and cheering that I felt like I was Maya. Maya Angelou that is. With the microphone now placed at my side, I raised my hand back up to my mouth and eyed Denim.

He looked me straight in my eyes as I did his and I said, "This was dedicated to you my love." Then I winked.

The host came up and I handed him the microphone as he said, "Wow now that's a sister with a voice. Denim did you inspire that piece?"

The host laughed and the crowd went into an uproar. I ran up to my sister who had her arms open for me to squeeze my way in and embrace her hug.

She screamed out, "You did that sis! You told that man off. Right there and in front of everyone."

"I sure did." We gave each other a high five as we made our way out of the lounge and onto the sidewalk laughing. I was on cloud nine. That was the night I became the woman I am today.

Chapter 1

Dahlia Jones

"Don't sit here and not tell me the entire scoop!"

I looked over Nitrah's shoulder and saw Charmaine walking out of her class. I waved her over and said, "Char you won't believe what Nitrah did last night without us."

Charmaine was a senior at the university. We had known her a year since she transferred from a school in North Carolina.

"What did I miss?" Char dropped her books on the bench where we sat and looked straight at Nitrah.

"Ok so Tierra took me to Soul Bounce, the poetry spot where Denim DJs on Thursday and Friday nights."

"Ugh! Are we mentioning him again?" Char interrupted.

"No Char listen. Let Nitrah finish."

"Well I performed This little game we play."

I grinned from ear to ear. "That's my girl. I can't believe you did that right in front of Denim either."

"Why not? It was for him. That was a bold move girl, but I am proud of you." Charmaine added. "So what did Denim do?"

"Nothing, but he was embarrassed. He knew I was talking about him and then when I openly told him that the poem was dedicated to him I could see red steaming from his eyes. Plus the host laughed and rubbed it in. He was the laughing stock of the lounge."

I added, "So you sure you don't want to get back with Denim? I mean y'all been together since high school."

"Dahlia I got a number last night. Cameron is his name. And I am going to go out with him tonight." Nitrah overlooked my question.

Charmaine laughed and said, "I guess that means she's moving on Dahlia." I laughed too and gave Nitrah a high five.

"Well, let me get to my next class and I will meet y'all over at the dorms by six tonight."

"Didn't I tell you I am meeting up with Cameron?" Nitrah winked before hopping up and walking away. I laughed as I hugged Char goodbye and went to class.

Chapter 2

Charmaine Wright

She was knocked out in one of her drunken stupors so I rolled her over on her side. The stench that rose from the opening of her mouth gripped the walls of my stomach and it jerked into full out agitated convulsions that I wanted to vomit, but I clinched my nose really tight with my index and thumb to fight the funk.

"Greta!" I knew yelling was useless. She couldn't hear a word that came out of my mouth.

I stepped directly over her body and walked towards the linen closet. I pulled out blanket and tossed it over her. Just then I heard a knock on the door.

"Who is it?" I was hoping it wasn't one of the sorry ass men Greta always had running up and through here. Sometimes I wished I could afford to live on campus in the dorms with Nitrah and Dahlia, but since that wasn't the case I was stuck with my mother, Greta the drunk.

"Babe it's me. Open up." A smiled emerged across my face as I rushed towards the door. I swung it open and jumped in his arms.

He leaned down to kiss me back and asked, "How was class babe?" Then he tapped my ass before moving me to the side to walk in. He immediately saw Greta on the floor.

"Oh babe don't worry about Greta. She's drunk again. Go on back to my room and I will make you something to eat."

Tim turned around and looked at me in disgust. "I can't stand her drunken ass. You want me to move her or something?"

"Tim just go to the back. I got this, ok?" I was borderline aggravated and embarrassed, but Tim had been my boyfriend for six months, he knew how Greta was.

I was the only child she had. After I left North Carolina I moved to Chicago for a while and then here to Fort Worth. To say I had it ruff was an understatement. From an absent mother, nonexistent father, multiple rapes from family members and boys in the neighborhood leaving North Carolina was a must to survive. Greta tracked me down and cried all the tears she could cry about not having anywhere to go. So I let her stay with me. I didn't want her to stay seeing as though she could never stay off the bottle or with one man that was good for her. Growing up, two of her boyfriends use to have sex with me when she was passed out. I knew more then I needed to know about sex by the time I was nine years old.

I had been on my own since I was 14. Just me and my best friend, Monica, who stayed behind in Chicago She stayed for love and I left in search for some. I found it in Tim. He was good enough in my book. I've had my share of bad men too. I learned how to pick the worst men to be with from Greta's bad track record. Tim on the other hand, wasn't so bad. He was in school, handsome, spent time with me, and for me that was enough to label him as one of the best I ever had.

"Fine whatever. I want some fried chicken so either make it or go get it." He stepped over Greta and walked down the hallway to my room. Shoot I don't have any chicken. I walked over to my purse to rummage through it. It was Wednesday and I didn't get paid from my waitressing job until Friday. I found ten dollars. That had to last me for lunch at school.

"Hurry up!" I heard Tim yell out.

I weighed my options in my head and decided to go get Tim a two piece meal from the chicken spot around the corner. I yelled out, "Babe I will be back in ten minutes. I am going to go get us some chicken."

"Yeah whatever," he replied.

I walked my route to the chicken place with my last ten dollars stuffed in my pocket. Tim's meal was $7.78. That meant I only had enough to get one chicken leg for me. I decided to save my change and cook myself some Ramen noodles at the house. As long as Tim got what he wanted I was ok with not eating.

Chapter 3

Nitrah Hill

I had on some of the shortest shorts I could think of. My sister Raven helped me pin my hair up in a bun. I had on some red Converse that were folded down to my ankles and a red fitted t-shirt. Cameron was taking me to the movies to see "The Best Man" and then dinner afterwards.

Cameron reached down and grabbed my hand as we made our way to the Sundance Theatre downtown. On the weekends in Fort Worth, a lot of young couples came to this theatre.

"You look nice tonight Nitrah."

I blushed and said, "Cam you look good too. What's that you have on? You smell good." I leaned in to smell the base of his neck. He smiled.

"Don't do that woman." He laughed and dodged my attempt to lean in closer.

I smirked and innocently asked, "What are you talking about?"

"Oh there you go trying to act innocent. You got some nerve. You better be glad I love dark meat." He licked his lips and smiled.

I rolled my eyes in laughter. I was chocolate as many would say. Although, I was always complimented on the dark smooth look of my skin, it wasn't until my senior year in high school that I even liked the color of my skin.

"Ok Cam, come on so you can woo me with this dinner and a movie." I pulled on his arm as we made our way to the ticket booth and into the theater. I was excited to be on a date for once without the slightest thought of Denim.

ððð

We left Razzoos Seafood Restaurant and were now walking the streets of downtown Fort Worth. The spring breeze danced around my skin causing a slight shiver. I entwined my fingers in Cameron's and listened to him tell me about the football game he played last week. It was new for me to date an athlete. Shoot it was new for me to date anyone besides Denim.

"Enough about me talking off your ear. What about you Nitrah, you're in school for what again?" He asked.

"I'm an English major. I love everything books and poetry." I laughed to myself and continued, "You know I performed at Soul Bounce just the other day."

"Performed?" Cameron quizzed. His deep dimples sunk further into his cheeks as he smiled with excitement. He was genuinely enjoying what I was talking about.

"Yeah my sister, Tierra, convinced me to recite this poem I had written in public. It was my first time."

"So you write too. Hmm that's sexy on a woman." He joked as he leaned in and pecked my lips with his. He then looked behind me and said, "Let's go in there."

I turned around to see where he was looking. "Barnes & Noble?"

He had started pulling me by my arm and leading me in the direction of the book store. "Yeah why not? You can show me some of the books you have been reading."

Trailing behind him like a shy school girl I asked, "You don't mind going in here?"

Finally across the street Cameron stopped and looked at me. "What do you mean? Sure come on, should be interesting to see what men bashing books you are reading." He laughed and took my hand again leading me into the book store.

After grabbing a couple of smoothies from the café we made our way up the elevator to the fiction section. My section. I loved coming in here finding new books to read. I immediately searched for some of my favorites. Grabbing a Kimani romance book, I turned around and pushed it into Cameron's chest, "Read this." I laughed.

He took it into his hands and frowned, "Oh naw ma! I am not reading chick lit. I need a man's book."

I giggled and threw my head back laughing. Cameron laughed with me. I suddenly heard a familiar laugh. But I knew I was tripping. No way was I hearing who I thought I heard. Cameron noticed my mood change.

"Nitrah are you ok?"

I heard the voice say, "No babe you look good reading this one." Then he laughed. I frowned as I noticed it was a genuine happy laugh. It wasn't forced or anything.

I threw the book that I had in my hand down and stomped around the bookshelf to confirm that it was who I thought it was. I could feel Cameron close behind me as I was now facing Denim with his current lay of the week.

"Well..." I said with my arms folded across my chest.

Denim turned around and jumped away from me. The anger was steaming through my vessels and it felt like my pupils were going to burst. Cameron walked up to me and sized Denim up giving him a head to toe assessment.

"Denim Overton," Cameron said. They knew each other mutually from the university.

"Cameron Stone. Nitrah Hill. Ummm what's up?"

The woman with him pushed her way in between Denim and I and said, "And I am Patrice."

I ignored her as my line of questioning began, "Were you forced to come in here tonight? I mean you seem awfully cheery to be in a place I use to have to drag you into."

"Forced, no mama Denim here begged me to come. After dinner he wanted to show me some of the books he was reading. Isn't that right baby?" Patrice turned around and rubbed Denim's chest in a seductive manner.

I was so angry I didn't realize the tears that were forming in my eyes. "You brought her here?" I scrunched my nose up at Patrice and gave her an expression that said she held a funky odor. Bitch ain't cuter than me.

9

I had loved Denim since I was a kid in high school, but we had known each other since grade school. I had known him my entire life and all of my life I had to force him to be a part of what I loved and that was reading. He hated to go in the book stores and roam the shelves with me, hated to go to poetry readings, he hated to read the long love letters I wrote. But now he was standing here with another woman doing the things with her that I always wanted him to do with me.

"I mean Nitrah we were just walking by and came in," Denim said attempting to sound innocent.

I turned to Cameron and grabbed his hand, "I'm ready to go Cam."

Cameron gladly took my hand after throwing Denim a look I knew was a warning and led me out of the store. I didn't have much else to say as we hopped in Cameron's car. I was heartbroken. Years of being devoted to a cheating man like Denim only for another woman to get what I had always wanted.

Chapter 4

Dahlia

I threw myself on my bed and stuffed my face deep within my pillow. My dorm mate was playing some annoying ass music, "Shan please cut that shit down." I yelled through pillow.

"What you don't like?" Her Asian tone was already working my nerve and I hadn't been in my room but five minutes. Just shut the hell up.

I heard a knock on the door and Shan went over to open it. "Oh hey Eric, Dahlia in a bad mood today," she chuckled and said in her robotic voice as she walked out the door. I turned over to see my boyfriend Eric walking towards me.

He bent down and kissed me on my lips, "That Shan is aight with me." He laughed knowing good and well I couldn't stand her.

"Hey what's up? What are you doing over here?"

"Came to see what you were doing? I saw Charmaine at the dance off. She said you were probably in your room."

"Yeah, I had planned on going, but I had to study for my exam in the morning. Plus Nitrah is out on a date. So I just chilled. Who was Char with?"

"Some dude I ain't seen before. But anyway you want to go grab something eat before I got to head back to my room?"

I rose up agreeing to get something to eat and began to grill him on what the guy Charmaine was with looked like.

"Ask her Dahlia. I ain't getting in it," Eric said refusing to dish any scoop.

"Well damn. I was just wondering. Shoot, she keeps everything such a secret." He changed the subject asking about the fish fry we were having over my mom's house next weekend.

"Just bring your appetite love. And tuff skin, my whole family will be there."

He laughed and assured me that he could handle himself.

Chapter 5

Nitrah

I walked over to Cameron's couch and plopped down. I had a headache, but I did not want him to notice. I wasn't aggravated from anything he was doing anyway so I wanted to make sure I kept up my ok persona. But I wasn't ok. Denim always tended to get under my skin. The say never date your friends anyway, but no I just had to go and fall in love with my childhood friend.

Cameron walked back over to me after placing down a glass of cranberry juice. I took a long drink and let the cold liquid settled in my stomach. I sat the glass back down on the table and pressed backwards onto the couch once again.

"You ok?" Cameron asked.

"Yeah I'm fine Cam; let's not talk about what we both think I am tripping over ok?"

He nodded his head, bent down and grabbed my left foot and placed it in his lap. "Bring your other leg up too." He gestured. So I did.

He unstrapped my sandals and I allowed my head to fall back on the sofa's pillows. Cam's hands were wrapped around my feet one at a time giving me the massage generated from heaven. His hands were soft for an athlete who lifted weights every other day. To top that off, he gave me the perfect pressure on my feet. Hmmm if he can rub my feet like this I wonder...

I laughed at the thought.

"What's funny?" Cameron's voice was low and seductive, and it scared the hell out of me. I jerked my head upward to face him.

"What?"

"You laughed!"

I covered my mouth with my hand. "I didn't realize I laughed out loud."

He smirked giving me his million dollar smile. Sexy couldn't define a man like Cameron. He was so damn pretty, way prettier than most guys I am attracted to. But funny thing was, his looks didn't match his personality. You would expect a man like him to be conceited, arrogant, and have huge expectations from a woman. But he didn't. He was a gentleman. I liked him a lot.

I almost sound like a shy schoolgirl when I whisper, "I was just thinking."

Cameron was now rubbing my calves as he says, "Oh yea about what?"

I took a deep breath and blew it out as of Cameron's hands trailed across my feet, then my calves, to now squeezing and rubbing my thighs.

"Ummm, I don't know." I mumble. Our eyes were locked in on one another. Each of us daring not to blink or look away. Our breathing shared the same pattern. You could clearly see the rise and fall of our chest as deep orgasmic breaths escaped us. My bottom lip began to shake from pure desire. I couldn't manage to speak or look away for that matter.

Cameron had me lost in his sexual stare. With no words spoken, we read each other's minds. The muscles in my legs pulsed as he meticulously gripped my thighs and his thumbs grew nearer and nearer to his final destination. Slightly parting my legs I felt a rush of heat escape from there creating sweat beads on my brow.

It was hot. It felt like I was in a sauna. I couldn't breathe, my chest got tighter and tighter as each second passed.

Cameron was towering over me now. His hands trailed up my ass to my lower back as he scooted me down to be completely under him. Still with nothing said between us he leaned in and kissed me.

You would have thought this was the first time. Our first kiss. But it wasn't. I had kissed Cameron several times before. But with this kiss he was making a statement. Creating a landmark right on the curves of my lips. Moving in slowly and then quickly placing kisses on each lip as they slightly parted.

When a moan escaped his mouth, my desire to feel him inside of me set off an explosion. My panties were now saturated with my juices. If you were to squeeze them with your bare hands a river of my juices would trail down your hand. I pulled Cameron on top of me as our kisses deepened.

Squeezing the back of his head with one hand, I take my free hand in search for what could ease my desire.

He buried his face into the depths of my neck and the heat from his heavy breathing pushed me even further to the edge. I trailed my hand down in search of his hardness. I gripped his long hardened shaft and bit my bottom lip. His zipper was piercing my hands as I squeezed him harder. He jerked in my hand.

As I unzipped his pants I moaned, "I need to feel you." After reaching in his pocket for that golden package, he swiftly pulled his pants down. I smiled at the sight of gold. I had already felt what I knew was a gold mine, but watching him apply our protection only made me wetter.

His dick was perfection. Thick and blackened with the right amount of pink just at the tip of his head. I sucked and licked my bottom lip wondering if I should taste a sample of him before we went all the way. I nearly shivered as I watched it bounce from side to side as he made sure our protection was perfect. And boy was it perfect.

Cameron looked back up towards me taking his attention back to my lips. I gently slide my red lace thongs to my ankles and kicked my leg over my head tossing them across the room. As I went to let my leg back down Cameron grabbed it in midair, pushed upward, and with one hard thrust entered me. I felt my juices as they began to squeeze out from the creases of my lips onto the couch cushions.

I threw my head back into the seat and screamed out as he pushed in further. My eyes rolled into the back of my head and my entire body went limp as I instantly began to convulse with pleasure. Quickly I felt the beginning of my orgasm as Cameron's motions were matching the desire I needed to climax.

"You like this big dick?" Oh, he's a dirty talker huh? I couldn't talk because I was too caught up from the pressure of him entering into my deep end so I gave him a head nod. He leaned down and sloppily kissed my lips and asked the question again, this time with another hard deep thrust.

I screamed, "Yes, I love this big dick!" I couldn't take it. My mind was going crazy, I couldn't literally see as my orgasmic eruption was nearing its end. When I screamed out I that I was coming Cameron began to go faster. He raised up my other leg and began hammering in and out as quickly as he could.

"Oh shit Nitrah I am about to come!" He yelled out. I grabbed my legs using them as my safety belt as this ride I was on was about to take a major drop. I squeezed my pelvis really tight, closed my eyes, and bit my bottom lip so hard it pierced my skin.

Cameron and I exhaled at the same time. I let my legs fall as my breathing stayed rapid. Cameron plopped down on top of me as his chest moved in and out on top of mine. I laughed out loud and said, "Wow!"

Cameron matched my laugh, lifted his head off of my chest and asked, "Are you ready for round two?"

I smiled like a school age girl and said, "For that big dick. Getty up!"

Chapter 6

Dahlia

I grabbed a red cup full of beer and made my way through the crowd. My brother, Zachary, was playing The Isley Brothers, that old people's soul music.

Over the music I heard my little sister's voice, "Zach where's the music like the bump and grind?" I rolled my eyes and walked over to her.

"Joyclyn why aren't you in your room like I asked you to?"

"Girl boom, I ain't going to my room. I can party with the big dogs now." My sister was fresh out of high school and thought she could hang out with us. She eyed my red cup and I snatched it away.

"Look away Miss Thang. This is for my boo Eric. No drinking. Go get a soda."

She laughed and walked away as I went in search for Eric to hand him his drink. Mama was at work but she didn't mind us having a fish fry there. I occasionally threw gatherings just because this time my older brother came over with his current boo of the week. I didn't complain about him bringing another random chick into Mama's house seeing as though I would throw parties even when Mama asked me not to.

I found Eric cornered up with a random chick I didn't even know. After the initial thought of who the hell invited her to my Mama's house I began to wonder why the hell she was so close into Eric's face and why he was grinning from ear to ear. I walked over and cleared my throat. They separated like roaches when the lights are suddenly turned on.

I extended my hand to give him his drink clearly displaying an attitude and said, "Here." The girl walked away, but not before I gave her a head to toe assessment. "And she was?"

"Oh come on babe don't go acting all jealous." Eric leaned in sloppily kissed my cheek then took the beer.

Rolling my eyes before walking off I said, "Don't go choking on a fish bone tonight." I acted as if I was running a knife across my throat. Testing and warning him at the same time to not flirt with another chick in my face. He laughed and waved me off.

I turned on my heels to go find my girls. I wanted to avoid a confrontation with Eric the Mack.

I saw Nitrah and Charmaine at the kitchen table playing cards and laughing it up. I walked over to join them. "What is the current scoop?"

Nitrah giggled and picked up her drink to avoid the question.

I eyed her and said, "Is this about the guy Eric seen Char with the other day?"

Charmaine took her hand to her chest and pretended to be innocent. "What guy?"

"Don't go there with me Char; you know good and well what I am talking about." I gave her the evil eye.

"Ugh nosey. We were talking about Nitrah's bump and grind with sexy ass Cameron. Not me and this pretend guy you are speaking of." Charmaine held plenty of sarcasm in her voice, but as soon as she said "bump and grind" my attention was now on Nitrah.

"You slut!" I laughed out.

Nitrah covered her mouth to hide her obvious smile. "Girl it was ooo wee good."

I leaned in and whispered, as if anyone could hear me over the music anyway, "Was it?" I was dying to hear the details. "Why y'all heifas didn't call me over before y'all start spilling the juice? That's some straight bull."

They laughed when Nitrah said, "I didn't get to the good part." My eyes were watching Nitrah's mouth so I didn't see the obvious change in her demeanor until Char grunted. I looked over to Charmaine and then followed her eyes behind me. Damn, Denim just ruined the opportunity for me to hear some gossip.

Chapter 7

Nitrah

Bad timing. Bad timing. Must I say again bad timing? "Dahlia did you invite him here?" I eyed her.

She shrugged her shoulder and said, "Well he must have remembered when I mentioned it to him last month. But y'all were trying to work it out then."

Charmaine added, "What negro remembers an invite from a month ago? He has to have a motive."

I rose up and walked over to Denim. It didn't help that he was looking just as handsome as he wanted to be. Nope that didn't help at all. I put some extra swing into my step just to make him squirm. I knew I was looking extra cute tonight anyway.

Walking up to him I said, "Denim."

He casually bent down, kissed my forehead, and said, "Nitrah."

I looked around him searching for his current lay of the week, "Where is she?"

He smirked. I hated that. He had this cute dimple on his left cheek that I always loved to stick my finger into and just tease him about. It really wasn't a dimple. When we were around ten years old a kid brought a bow and arrow to school. While he was playing around it went off and shot out straight for Denim's face. It went through his cheek. He had to get 15 stitches. In the end he had a scar that looked like a dimple.

"Where is who Nitrah?"

"Your bitch," I blurted. I was mad at myself for saying it once it came out. I didn't want Denim to see that I was hurt. That I was mad that he was doing things with her that he refused to do with me. I had been his best friend since grade school, I was his girl, I was his lover, and I was supposed to be his everything. Denim wasn't anything but a hoe in the end.

"A little angry aren't we." He was antagonizing me. So much that I visualized myself punching him in his gut.

I switched my weight from one hip to the other and folded my arms. I wasn't in the mood for games. I hadn't seen him since the Barnes & Noble incident. I hadn't returned his calls either. And now here he stood in front of me in Dahlia's mom's house. Yeah, he came here looking for me. So I know he wouldn't dare bring another woman in here. Not with my girls here to beat her ass down.

"I came to see you." Denim said, interrupting my thoughts.

"I'm sure you did." He extended his hand and begged with his eyes for me to take it. I didn't look back at my girls even though I knew they were watching.

"Five minutes," I said. I took his hand and followed him out the door. But not before I heard Dahlia yell, "I'm right here if we need to beat that ass Denim." I laughed out loud loving the craziness my friend possessed.

Chapter 8

Charmaine

The night was young. It was only ten o'clock, but I had a test in the a.m. I had to hurry home and get some sleep if I was going to pass it with a clear mind. I pulled up into my apartment complex and shut my car off. It wasn't the prettiest thing but it got me to school, work, and home. I cringed at the thought of home. I didn't want to go in there.

Hopefully Greta was sleep. As I made each step up to my door on the second floor I was regretting whatever was going to happen on the other side of it.

I unlocked the door and pushed it open. The TV was on as I walked in, but it was fuzzy with no signal. It was dark. Not one light was on.

"Greta!" I called out but heard nothing.

Still buzzed from the alcohol I consumed earlier I shrugged my shoulders, hit the power button on the TV, and went in route to my room to take a hot shower. I pulled my shirt over my head and flipped on my room light.

I tossed my purse onto my bed and followed it. I plopped down on the mattress and began to undo my sandals. The quiet serene sound throughout the apartment was eerie. I didn't want to admit that I was a little uneasy in my own home.

What is Greta doing? Tossing both of my shoes onto the floor I rose up in search of my usually drunken mother. The house looked just the way I had left it. Other than a half-eaten sandwich on the end table, not one thing was out of place.

The apartment was so quiet that I could hear the cracks of the floor underneath my feet with each step I took. I blew out air as I realized I was creeping my own self out. It was just like one of those scenes in a horror movie when the helpless woman follows the noise and then gets attacked. I balled up my fist in preparation for a fight if I needed to get down.

"Greta!" I called out again. I knew calling her name was a waste of time. It was night time so it mainly meant one thing; she was drunk and knocked out.

Finally at her doorway I pushed open her cracked door. Her TV was on and as my eyes trailed across the room I noticed she was sprawled across her bed. Walking over to her I yelled out, "Get your ass up and wash up or something. It stinks in here." I squeezed my nose shut because as I neared the odor from her body intensified.

She lay across her bed only in a torn shirt and panties. Her small frame was still, pale, and once again I felt like she was wasting away her day. All Greta did was drink and collect a disability check. I wanted so badly for her to just return to North Carolina and leave me alone.

I bent down over and nudged her on her shoulder. She didn't move. I felt a sense of an eerie cold breeze run over my right arm across my shoulders and down my back. Something wasn't right. My voice now only above a whisper, "Greta!"

Nothing.

My heart beat began to beat faster and I unknowingly began to breathe deeper in and out as the unthinkable was running through my mind. She laid there lifeless. Lifeless.

I blinked multiple times slowly as I stared at the back of her head. I haven't seen the rise of her back go in and out yet. She was still. Dead as can be. I reached down and grabbed her left shoulder and with one hard lift I turned her over. My voice caught in the pits of my throat and I jumped back. Her eyes were so dark. Darker than anything I have ever seen before.

I didn't know what to do. I was afraid and disgusted at the same time as the smell of her vomit and feces began to permeate the entire room. I ran to the bathroom and I threw myself onto the toilet and released all the contents of my stomach.

Collapsing backwards onto the floor I began to cry. I cried harder than I had since leaving North Carolina as a teenager. I had ran away from there to escape a brutal rape and now it seemed I would have to run away from here to escape the damage Greta had caused. And now even in her death she haunted me with the never ending memories of pain she has caused. Death was to give you freedom right, but now all I had left was anger towards a woman that wasn't even here. She had escaped hell on Earth but I was still suffering from the damage she had done to me.

It had to have been hours before I made my way off of the bathroom floor. I stood up in front of the mirror and stared my reflection. Her eyes, my eyes were heavy, swollen, and empty. I had cried many days from being a motherless child. Although Greta was there she wasn't there. Not unless she was turning tricks in the bedroom right next to mine, snorting coke down her nose and following it up with a bottle of beer, or hinting to me that she wanted to teach me how to turn tricks.

I hated her with a passion.

I said out loud, "She deserves to be thrown away with the trash." And as if a light bulb went off, I figured that would be my departing ceremony for her. I rushed into the kitchen and grabbed as many trash bags as I could. I pulled out a bottle of bleach and put on some plastic gloves from underneath the kitchen sink. Last I pulled out the largest suitcase I could find in the hall closet. Greta's coffin. The perfect goodbye.

Chapter 9

Nitrah

I turn over onto my side to stretch only to be stopped by a rock hard body. I jumped up with my eyes bulging out and yelled, "What the hell?"

I stared at the back of Denim's head for what seemed like an eternity. What and when did this happen? I was naked. I raised the sheets up and looked over my naked body and glanced over and saw Denim's naked ass. Oh no I didn't.

How in the hell did this man end up in my bed for the umpteenth time? I fell back and threw my hand over my head and started to shake it as if I was telling myself no. But it was too late I had done the okie doke. This man had done it to me again. All I remember was us talking at Dahlia's mom's house and having a few drinks. Oh yea we did end up kissing too. That I do remember. But now I am in my bed naked with this negro. He must be my weakness.

You are the weakest link. I subconsciously rose up and looked around my room for something I could throw at Denim's head. Nothing harder than a pillow so I decided to just hit him with my fist.

"Ahhh!" Denim jumped up grabbing the spot I hit him in. "Nitrah what the hell?"

"What are you doing in my apartment Denim?" My eyes couldn't help but to travel this is bouncing dick as it jerked with each step he took back and forth. My eyes darted back and forward back and forth until I grew dizzy.

"What the hell do you mean? I drove us here last night remember." He plopped back on his side of my bed and stared at me with a raised eyebrow. I darted my eyes from his head to his other head.

"You did?" My voice held a hint of innocence and embarrassment as I tried to pretend like we both didn't know I was eyeing his dick like a fat kid wanting a piece of cake.

"Nitrah, what's up? You are tripping this morning?" My eyes bulged out of my head once he said morning. I knew I had an exam today and I had to take it or else I would be begging for extra credit.

Jumping up out of the bed I yell, "I have Professor Wilkes' exam in thirty minutes Denim. Ugh!" I ran my fingers through my hair that was clearly mangled and blew out hot air. I rushed into the bathroom and turned the water on. I reach for my CD player and pressed play. Heather Headley began to flow "In My Mind". Stripping down to nothing I stepped in and allowed the water to take away the funk and the evidence of last night's escapades with Denim.

Ten minutes later I was grabbing a towel and wrapping it around my body when I heard, "Here she comes."

Raising an eyebrow I call out, "Denim?" It didn't sound like his voice so I don't know why I asked anyway. But

I did. Not getting a response I dried off quickly and wrapped the towel around my body. I walked into my room and found it empty so I quickly slipped on my panties and bra and grabbed a sundress to slip on.

"Denim!" I called out again.

This time he replied, "In the living room"

I grabbed my lotion and walked out of my room. What I saw made me drop the lotion and gasp. "Hey Cam what are you doing here?" I was busted. It was written all over my face. Then again I didn't expect my current boyfriend to be sitting in my living room in the early hours of the morning across from my ex. What was he doing here?

Denim's demeanor was un-phased. He sat there at the edge of my couch and looked directly at me as if he was waiting on a show to begin. It was clear that he had let Cameron in and knew good and well that this was going to be a sticky situation.

Cameron spoke first, "So is there anything you need to tell me?"

I opened my mouth to say something but nothing came out. My eyes went from Denim as I hinted for him to help me out, but he was a lost cause. "Cam... umm no... I don't have anything to say." I walked over to where he stood and looked him directly in the eyes. I wanted to try to be as honest as possible. My eyes darted towards Denim, "I do have something to say to you though... Let yourself out.""

Denim raised his hands up in surrender with the ugliest smirk on his face. As he grabbed his keys and opened my door he said, "Call me later on babe." He walked out and shut the door behind him. Asshole!

Cameron looked at the closed door then back to me, "Babe?"

Denim had said that to totally upset Cameron. His dirty ass cheated on me and now has the audacity to screw up a perfect relationship I had with Cameron. I guess I couldn't blame it all on him. I allowed Denim back into my bed.

Cameron stared at me halfway confused and disgusted. His eyes alone cause me to feel smaller than a mouse. "Cam!" I whispered. "I am not going to stare you in the eye and start a baby please speech. I'm wrong. I was weak. He does that to me sometimes. It's like he knows how to get to me."

"That's not what I want to hear Nitrah. How do you think I feel about that?" He stepped backwards from me placing his hands in his pockets. Damn he was a good one and I knew that even more as I stared at him and became even more disgusted with myself for allowing Denim to have me. It's like he gets a free fuck Nitrah card each time.

"I don't know," I replied.

"I can't be with someone who is obviously still in love with someone else. Are you telling me that you can't say no to him? That you just can't be with me?"

I lowered my head as if I was a child and said, "I can resist him. I just don't know if I am all the way there yet."

I heard Cameron grunt a little as he switched his weight from one foot to the other. "I get it. We're young and shit. I don't expect you to marry me and we have this commitment. But damn Nitrah I do expect respect and I

31

can't respect this. I can't openly compete with a lifelong relationship you got with that nigga." He was yelling now. I jerked at the sound of his heavy tone. He was angry. I couldn't blame him for that.

"You shouldn't have to. And you won't. Give me some time to just make it right."

Cameron walked up to me placing his hands on my shoulders and said, "Baby you can't get rid of a life time friend like that. I can't compete for a spot in your heart that's bigger than his. I'm sorry." Kissing my temple. He released my shoulders and began to walk away.

My voice cracked with emotion as I asked, "You're walking away from me?"

He stopped turned around and said, "I'm sure when you're done with playing games with him and every other nigga you'll let me know when you are ready."

In a few measly steps he opened my front door and was gone. I wanted to break down and cry but the clock quickly reminded me that I had an exam to take. I grabbed my back pack, purse, and phone, and pretended that this morning wasn't going to cause me to fail this test.

Chapter 10

Dahlia

Homecoming time was the best. I loved the football games, the State Fair, and the concerts that always came into town around this time of the year. It meant one thing: eye candy. And my eyes were seeing a lot of sweet something's walking around. I felt a push on my back which interrupted my current thoughts.

"Heifer pay attention." Charmaine pointed ahead of me as we were walking around the fair grounds and I realized I was getting ready to walk into a booth.

I heard Nitrah laughing behind me I turned around and rolled my eyes. "Whatever. Your ass would be near collision too if you were paying attention to all these fine men out here."

"Girl please. I am good." Nitrah turned her attention to the booth that was serving popcorn. Charmaine noticed Nitrah's lack of interest in the men too.

"Are you still on a man hiatus? It's been four weeks already." Charmaine asked.

Walking away from us and to the booth she said, "I just want some popcorn."

"Yea right." I said stomping my feet trying to speed up my walk to catch up to her.

At the booth Nitrah ordered, "Give me two bags please."

"Two bags?" I asked.

Nitrah laughed and said, "Yeah it's for you two heifers so y'all want be sticking y'all stank hands in mine."

I snatched the bag out of her hand and took and huge hand full of popcorn just to get on her nerves. "It's good too," I mumbled.

Behind us we heard a voice said, "Hey Nitrah!"

All three of us turned around and our eyes landed on a young girl. My initial thought was that she was cute, but obviously young. She looked like she still was in high school.

Nitrah walked over to her and gave her a hug, "Hey Ms. Lady. What are you doing here?"

She hugged her back and told her that she was leaving Texas Wesleyan, which was a university on the East side of Fort Worth, and would be going to the university with us next semester..

Half way through their conversation Nitrah remembered Char and I were standing there and said, "Oh hey y'all this is Jazzaray. She was in the transfer office yesterday."

Char extended her hand first and said, "Jazzaray. I like your ghetto fabulous name." We all laughed.

Jazzaray laughed with us and said, "Oh just call me Jazz. Y'all go to the university too?"

We replied yes as she complimented us on our outfits and then asked who we were all hanging with tonight. "It's just us. Who are you hanging out with?"

"It's just me. I wanted to come out but one of my girls punked out on me. So here I am rocking solo."

Nitrah cupped her arm and signaled for Char to cup her other arm and said, "You a part of the three amigo's now. What ride y'all want to get on first?"

I yelled out as I cupped Nitrah's arm so we would all be linked together. "Anything that turns me upside down." That day we had a hell of a time. We rode every carnival ride you could think of. I got a few numbers too, but tossed them away declaring to be faithful to Eric.

That night Jazz was joined to our hip. My circle of three became a circle of four.

ððð

I met up with Charmaine at Lola's Coffee House on campus to study for an exam we both had to take in Geography. Not that I didn't like this spot because every now and then the place would be packed with eye candy. But it was raining so there weren't too many guys to look at. One thing I liked to do when it rained was nothing. But here I was.

I spotted Charmaine at a table sipping on coffee. I walked up to her and hugged her from behind, "Hey mama!"

She pushed her head back into my chest and embraced my hug saying, "Hey lady, about time you got here."

I sat down and threw my back pack on the ground. "You better be glad I made it out in this mess. Look at what the rain did to my hair." I pointed out the frizzy ends of my hair as Charmaine laughed and waved her me off.

"I am on the first page. Open your book so we can get out of here in two hours." I did what I was told and after I ordered myself some coffee I was nose deep into my studies as well.

It was maybe forty-five minutes later when I heard Charmaine's stomach growl. Laughing I say, "Hungry aren't we."

Charmaine gave a look of embarrassment before she said, "Girl I didn't get a chance to eat this morning. Just this coffee and muffin."

"Greta's butt ain't cook you anything? That's the least she could do."

She nodded her head no. As I was prepared to open my mouth to speak a familiar face walked into the café and before I could hide my expression Charmaine turned around to see who it was I was looking at.

She turned around and raised an eyebrow. "You know him?"

I cleared my throat to hide the slight discomfort in it and said, "I know of him." Waving my hand to change the subject I say, "Let's not talk about it."

"Girl the way you acting, all I want to do is talk about it."

Charmaine stared at me for what seemed like an eternity when I said, "His name is Tim Meadows. He is the best friend to a guy I used to know."

"Troyon Washington?" Charmaine asked.

I was raised my eyebrow when I asked, "Yeah how do you know?"

"Well damn, I mean I have only been here from Chicago for a couple years, but I hear what's said on the streets. Troyon is this sexy ass heartbreaker. So I've heard. And Tim Meadows? Well I had a class with him and I know that he is friends with Troyon."

I leaned back in my seat just as Tim turned around. Our eyes locked and he gave me a head nod. "Oh yeah he remembers me alright from when I dated Troyon. Everyone calls him Troy though."

"Good he is leaving," I said as Tim walked out.

Charmaine interrupted my thoughts, "You dated Troyon?" Her question was a mixture of shock and curiosity.

It had been a few years since I had dated him and I had held this secret long enough from my girls. I finally decided to vent to her. "I dated Troy yes." I went on to tell her how we broke up after I learned I was an assignment for him pledging Kappa. He had filmed us having sex and showed everyone.

Charmaine dropped her mouth and said, "Wow and Tim knows this?"

I nodded my head yes.

Charmaine closed her text book and said, "Now I got to go eat. This mess just made my stomach turn into knots."

I reached out and grabbed Charmaine's hand and said, "Don't tell Nitrah and don't tell Jazz she just got into our circle. I don't want them knowing I was a sucker for Troy."

She nodded her head ok as we packed up and went in search for some food.

Chapter 11

Charmaine

I took one last glance at my now empty apartment and closed the door. I hopped in the U-Haul truck and drove it fifteen miles to my new apartment. I was still getting Greta's disability checks so I used one to put a deposit on a one bedroom spot closer to campus. I threw everything that she owned away in the garbage the same as I did her remains and didn't look back.

Stepping out of the truck I noticed Tim walking down the steps and said, "I figured you were on your way."

A little excited to see him I asked, "Are you here to help me move in?" He had refused to at first saying he had something else to do, but here he was and I was excited to see him want to help.

"I can grab a couple boxes while I am here." He casually said. He popped open the back door and proceeded to get a couple boxes. I directed him to get the heavy stuff.

"OK that's fine because my girls will be here and I know you don't want to be seen." I reminded him.

I followed behind him with a couple boxes of my own and unlocked the door to my apartment.

"Speaking of your girls, that's why I am here."

I dropped the boxes to my feet and went over to open the blinds in the place. "Yeah what's up?"

Tim continued, "I didn't know you knew Dahlia. She used to fuck with Troy."

"She told me."

"And I saw all of y'all at the carnival too and have been meaning to tell you to go ahead and solidify your new girl."

I turned and faced him and curiously asked, "Solidify?"

"Don't act like you don't know what the hell I am talking about."

I felt like I was a five year old girl being chastised as the green light went off in my head. "Jazz? You want Jazz?"

He nodded his head like what he was telling me was so natural. I wanted to yell no at the top of my lungs, but I never wanted to make Tim upset. This is the main reason why what he was asking me should be routine. I had brought many girls to him. Or I should say I brought them to us and allowed them in my bed with him. The man I loved. But now he was asking for my friend. Why?

"I can't have a threesome with my friend Tim. I love those girls. They are my only family."

"You won't be having a threesome. I want her as my main bitch."

I cocked my head to the side as I tried to hide my anger and pain. He refused to be with me in public, but was now staring at me in my face and telling me he not only still wanted me to be his secret but he wanted my friend to be his girl.

He walked out of my door, but not before saying, "Make it happen. Look I'll get a few more boxes but after that you're on your own. I got to go meet up with the fellas for a game of basketball."

As he walked out I then allowed the tears to fall down my face. I should bury him right next to Greta.

ð...ð

We were all piled over Nitrah's apartment for a girl's night in. Her sister's Tierra and Raven, Jazz, Dahlia, and I were all stuffed from Papa John's pizza and were now sprawled out on her floor.

"I swear they have the best Italian sausage," Jazz said.

I nodded my head in agreement as I threw my pillow below me to lay my head down. It was only a matter of time before everyone was fast asleep. I had struggled to go to sleep many nights since finding Greta dead in her own vomit. I had lied to the only couple folks who asked about her and eventually I'll let everyone know she left me yet again and I don't know where she went. Which in some part is true. I figured she was burning in hell.

I threw back my covers as the heat and anxiety from lack of sleep was started to take over my body. I got up and walked out onto Nitrah's patio. It was three in the morning and the Texas cool breeze was danced heavenly on my skin. I closed my eyes and threw my head to the sky.

My eyes jerked open when I heard, "You ok?"

"Dahlia, girl you scared me." She closed the patio door behind her.

"What are you still doing up?" She stood next to me at the railing and looked over me with concern. I must admit Dahlia was my girl; her, Jazz, and Nitrah. I loved them. But they didn't know half of my life. They didn't know I was born to a woman who loved the bottle more than me and who taught me how to trick off on a man so that I could get groceries for the house. They didn't know I ran away from North Carolina with my best friend Monica after we were ganged raped.

They didn't know I buried my mother's body and walked away as if I just threw away trash. I was tired of my life and I was trying to figure out why God gave me such a shitty one.

"A little insomnia," I said.

"Oh girl me too. I think I ate too late. That's my reason." Dahlia added.

I looked her over as she took her attention to the serene scenery of Nitrah's apartment complex and said, "Remember when you told me about Troyon?"

Her attention was set back on me now, "Yeah!" She said curiously.

"Have you ever wanted to get back at him for making that tape?"

She switched her weight to one leg and folded her arms, "Girl yeah, almost every day since it happened."

I swallowed before I said the next statement. I knew that what I was about to do would change the dynamics of my relationship with these girls forever. But I had a genius idea to help the man I loved get the girl he wanted, Jazz.

"I know a way to get him."

Dahlia laughed and said, "Do tell!"

"He broke your heart right? Well let's break his. With our best weapon." I turned my head and looked back into the apartment as Dahlia's eyes followed mine.

"Who are you looking at?" Dahlia asked.

"Nitrah is sexy, has that dark smooth chocolate skin. Every guy she talks to fall putty in her hand. She can train a guy like Troy.

"You want to use Nitrah to get to Troy? But she doesn't even know I use to date him."

"That is where we come in. We got to set up the scene. Finals are coming up and then graduation. After that we have plenty of time to get this thing rolling. Plus I am bored and need some excitement."

Dahlia leaned in with excitement and whispered, "What do you have planned?"

"I can ask Tim where they usually hang out. The four of us can meet and go out at the same time as them and allow nature to take its course. You of course will have to tell Nitrah and Jazz you use to date Troy and then ask her to play this little game of breaking his heart. My role will be the sound mind. Meaning I am going to be like I don't think this is a good idea. You know." I laughed. "I will play like I am innocent."

"What's Jazz and my role?" Dahlia asked.

"You will be the initiator. Confess your heartbreak and ask Nitrah to date Troy and make him fall for her. Jazz will be the friend who is in the mix. We will set up parties and dates and stuff like that for us all to hang out together. We will feed to Troy's friends that Nitrah really likes him and all that extra mess. Boys are easy to trick. I promise you Troy will finally get his heart broken."

Dahlia bites her bottom lip and said, "Man this is going to be a little tricky don't you think?"

"Not at all. But remember everyone must think you came up with this scam so that it can truly work out. I will always stick to my innocent role. Deal." I extended my hand and waited for Dahlia to take it.

She smiled and grabbed my hand, "Deal!"

"Alright girl let's go to bed. I am finally tired," I said. I followed Dahlia back in finally relieved to get the plan off of my chest. Before closing my eyes I grabbed my phone and text Tim.

Charmaine: Tim I got the plan in motion

Tim: Good job Char baby. I knew I could count on you

Charmaine: In no time you will be able to meet Jazz face to face

Tim: Muah

Charmaine: Night

Tim: Night babe

Ten Years Later

Chapter 12

Charmaine

I'm tripping right? This nigga just made love to my mind. Shit. This man just got into my head. I throw my head back into the pillow and exhale a breath I was holding for almost an hour. Damn an hour. I haven't had sex that long in, wait when was the last time? I tried to block out my past while I waited for him to come out of the bathroom. My mind was in overdrive.

I bit my bottom lip and laugh out just before he walks back in and lies down next to me and wraps his arms around my waist. I push my ass into him and wiggle backwards for a perfect fit.

"You have a beautiful body Charmaine." He whispered in my ear as his hands trail down my back to my thighs. I shivered trying to hide the anxiety he was creating. I wanted him badly. I wanted him more than anyone I've ever wanted. Why?

He held an addictive charm I needed a daily dose of. He dominated my every thought, he kissed me like I mattered, and he was powerful. As a matter of fact "power" should have been his name. He was in control of everything he touched, including me.

I didn't know he was going to be the death of me. Then again when you want something so much it can't all be good right? I was good however; until that day I told him no. He didn't like that word. And I had to learn the hard way and no one would even know I was gone. Not until it was too late.

Chapter 13

Nitrah

I looked Nina straight in the face and rolled my eyes. At nine, this girl was a smaller version of me. I swear she was the spitting image of who I am. I did not want to admit it but I was missing my baby being a baby. I had to admit I was a little annoyed about driving back home anyhow. So I was already on the edge of pissed off.

"Mama I just said he was cute dang." Nina sassed me with a slight attitude.

"I can't wait to get you out of this car and to your grandmother's." I heard her suck her teeth in. I looked in the back seat to see my four year old son, CJ, asleep. "Why don't you go to sleep like CJ did?" I barked at Nina.

"Mama this is the longest most annoying drive ever. " Nina was still going at my last nerve a mile a minute. We were driving in from Houston, where we now lived. I had been gone from Fort Worth since I became pregnant with CJ. Only coming to check in on the lounge that I owned in Fort Worth called the Lyrical Lounge.

Just as I opened my mouth to speak my phone rang. I laughed at the flashing of her name across my screen, "Ms. Jazzy Jazz how is we?"

"Nitrah where are you girl?"

"I am about thirty minutes away from the city limits of Fort Worth. I am almost home baby girl. You miss me?"

"This fourth of July celebration just got even crazier Nitrah."

"Huh? What do you mean?" Just as I heard Jazz open her mouth to speak the other line beeped. I saw his name and immediately started to try to put two and two together. The minute my old circle started to call my phone all at once I knew something wasn't right. My heart started to panic even before I realized it. I immediately pulled over to the side of the road and tried to ignore Nina asking if I was alright.

Before I clicked over and told Jazz to hold on; my mind started to race back to ten years ago. I was one of four best friends who ran the streets of Fort Worth. Fresh out of college my girls Jazzaray, Dahlia, and Charmaine were my rock. A lot had changed in ten years. Out of the four Jazzaray was my only friend from back in the day.

I had fallen in love with my best friend Dahlia's ex Troy and had a child, Nina with him. That was the beginning of the end. I swallowed hard as I said, "Jazz hold on Troy is on the other line."

I slowly pressed the other line as I braced myself. Him calling me at the same time as Jazz when I was only minutes away from Fort Worth couldn't be good. "Troy, hey what's up?

"Hey Nitrah how are you and the kids, are you close?"

"Yes only a few minutes away." Troy and I were on a good level now. We were actually good friends even after he

49

went back and had a relationship with Dahlia after I had Nina. But since Dahlia was long gone and had moved to Chicago it was easier for us to make up. But just like Jazz's tone, Troy's tone didn't sound so good either.

"Something is up isn't it?"

He paused before he said, "Come straight to my house Nitrah."

I paused as well and said, "Jazz is on the other line let me conference you in." I pressed the correct buttons to create a three way phone call and said, "Jazz are you there?" She replied. "Ok Troy is on the line. I know you both called me to tell me something right?" They didn't say a word. "I can tell by the both of your voices that something has happened. So tell me."

"Why don't you come into town first Nitrah?" Jazz added.

"Is it my Mama, my sisters, is it someone I know?" I started to yell out. I was annoyed and the long hours of driving didn't help either. I wanted them both to tell me what was really going on.

"Nitrah please calm down. You have Nina and CJ in the car." I glanced over to Nina who was listening with concern written all over her face.

I blew out air and wiped my eyes. "Just say the name and I am on the way."

"Troy why don't you say it, I just can't," Jazz mumbled.

"Ok Nitrah, let me know if I need me to come meet you. You have our babies in the car with you ok," Troy added. I agreed with him, but kept quiet. "Today we got a call from Tim." I made a mental note of the mention of Jazz's ex-husband and the father of her child. "It's Charmaine, Nitrah. She was found dead in Charlotte. She had been dead for over three weeks now."

My phone slowly slipped out of my hand as my eyes began to water with tears. I turned my head away from Nina and stared out of my window. I could see the city skylines of Fort Worth and began to sob. In that moment I was back into the city it was 2002 again. We were all together as friends, family, and happy. There was no drama. There was no pain. But the thought of one of us dying at the age of thirty-two never crossed my mind.

Charmaine was dead and the first thing I asked myself was how?

Chapter 14

Dahlia

I rolled my eyes at Joy who was dancing in the mirror as she tried on outfit after outfit. We were in town for my mother's wedding. Surprisingly she found love in some sixty-five year old man who went to her church and decided to have an over the top wedding. Otherwise I wouldn't be back in the hell hole I have come to know as Fort Worth, Texas.

"I am not going to sit here all day and watch you try out for America's Next Top Reject, now bring your ass on Joy." Joyclyn, my younger sister, turned to me and laughed.

"I look good for a twenty-seven year old huh?"

"No you look like shit. Now can we go?" I stood up from the dressing room chair and grabbed my purse. "That's a cute dress, get and let's go. I have somewhere to be."

Joy jerked her head around and laughed, "Where are you going? You haven't been home in over two years so who could you be possibly meeting up with?"

I opened my mouth to throw back a sarcastic remark when my cell phone rung. "Saved by the bell." I smirked clicking talk on its device. "Hey Monica! What's up?"

"I'm on my way to Texas." Monica's voice was low and dark. I held up a finger towards Joy hinting to give me a couple of minutes.

"Monica, what's wrong?" You may wonder why I was talking to Monica. The same chick who tried to mess up my former best friends Jazz's marriage. But after moving to Chicago myself, low and behold Monica was still here. Since I wasn't friends with Jazz or Nitrah any more I didn't see why it would be a problem to be her friend again. I was more shocked to see her still in Chicago after knowingly witness her and Char move around a lot.

"I got a call from Tim." She paused before continuing. "They found Charmaine." My body eased up as the sound of Charmaine's name on Monica's lips sipped out. It has been months since we had heard from Charmaine who went off to Charlotte supposedly with this guy she was in love with.

The word found didn't sound like good news to me. I immediately knew it was attached to something awful. "Found?"

"Yeah Dahlia. She's dead. He killed her. I just know he did!" Monica cried out. My heart was heavy. I knew I wasn't the best person in the world and had my own skeletons, but Charmaine was my friend. She had been Monica's friend since they were kids and now this.

"When will you be here?" I managed to say as heavy tears began to swell in my eyes. I noticed Joy walk over to me and placed her hand on my shoulder. I tried to watch her movements as Monica gave me notice on her arrival time. Charmaine's body as headed back to Texas.

I shut my phone off and dropped my head as I tried to hide back the tears that were blinding my eye sight. "Charmaine is dead." I cried out. Joy's mouth dropped in shock as she moved in closer to console me. I felt so guilty all of a sudden. I hadn't been the best friend to anyone in years including her and now she was gone. To make matters worse she was killed. That pained my heart most of all.

Chapter 15

Troyon Washington

I took a sip of the brown substance in my cup and swallowed hard. My nerves were shot and I knew I wouldn't calm down until I knew Nitrah was here with my daughter and her son. Safe and sound. My brother, Robert, had come over a mere half hour ago and was watching me like a hawk.

"Nitrah is responsible you know, she will get here in no time," he said.

"She should have been here already. Let me call Nina's cell phone." I said thinking that my daughter must be emotional right about now not knowing why her mother had broken down in front of her.

"Troy don't do that." Robert got up and placed his hand over mine. "Give her ten more minutes."

I nodded my head ok and sat back down only to hear the sound of tires making their way into my drive way. I rushed toward the door and pulled it open. Robert was steps behind me. I noticed Nitrah climb out of her SUV. Nina climbed out of the passenger seat and Nitrah's son Cameron jumped out and began to run towards me.

"Hey Pops!" He ran into my arms and my smile spread wide across my face. I dodged the plastic bat he had his grip on and planted a kiss on his cheek.

"Little man you sure are getting big. I can't be picking you up like this anymore. You're gonna kill my back." I leaned forward to act like my back was in pain as Cameron laughed out loud.

"CJ stop acting all hysterically over my daddy." Nina a spitting image of Nitrah stood before me. She was going into her teen years in a couple years and no doubt was too mature for her age if you asked me.

I sat Cameron down and playfully nudged Nina's head picking her up just as I did her brother. "You know Pops got enough kisses to go around." I planted kisses all over her face as she screamed for me to let her loose.

"Ugh Pops! I am too big for all of that. I'm hungry, what's there to eat?" She walked past me hugged her uncle and into the house she went.

I jogged over to Nitrah's car and looked her over. For a woman heading into her mid-thirties she didn't look a day over 25. Her dark skin was still blemish free and glowed. It looked like chocolate that had been melted with golden honey. Her long hair was blowing in the summer's breeze as she hid her true emotions behind the sunglasses she had planted on her face.

I looked back at Robert and asked him to get their luggage. "What, why? I am not staying here," Nitrah protested.

"Nitrah don't start with me." I laughed. I placed my hands on both of her shoulders and looked her in the face. I exhaled a breath of relief as I looked her over. She would always be this beautiful to me. She stared at me, her face solemn and peaceful.

"So I made it." Her voice as above a whisper and I heard a hint of pain in her tone. I forced myself to hold back any emotions I experienced while I was nervously waiting for her to pull up.

"Yeah, you made it." I reach towards her face with my right hand and began to move her sunglasses. I needed to see her eyes. As they became free she instantly began to lower her head. I brought it back up with the mere touch of my index finger. "I was worried about you."

"I'm a big girl Troy. I always manage to be ok." The sun brought out the cinnamon color in her eyes. I searched deep within them to call her bluff that she wasn't ok.

"Just pig headed," I joked.

"You may want to back up before your wife comes out and tries to scratch my eyes out."

I laughed a little and teased, "Those eyes, no I wouldn't let that happen. Come on into my mini palace. I'll show you where you are sleeping." I grabbed her hand and tried to lead her towards the house. It was a nice six bedroom house I had managed to afford now that I coached college basketball. Gabrielle had wanted this big house in preparation for when we had children together.

Nitrah tugged at my hand and looked at Robert who had luggage in his hand, "Robert tell this fool Gabrielle ain't gonna want me in her house."

"I ain't in it," Robert replied shrugging his shoulders.

"Did you ask Gabrielle if it was cool?" Nitrah asked.

"I'll tell her once she gets home. Now bring your ass woman." I tugged harder ripping her planted feet from their place.

"Ugh fine, but don't blame me when I listen attentively to y'all's argument tonight. You know she don't like me or understand why my son calls you Pops." Nitrah laughed harder then she should have as I waved her off.

"Woman just go lay down. I'll cook something for everybody tonight."

Inside Nitrah turned on her heels and raised an eyebrow, "Everybody?"

"Just those that you like." I leaned in planted a kiss on her cheek and popped her ass as she made her way up the stairs.

"Don't be hitting on me boy. You know I'm spoken for."

"Aren't we always?" I joked back. I went out to her car to help Robert with the rest of her and the kid's bags.

Chapter 16

Jazzaray Wayne

I rolled over to Maxwell's side of the bed and stretched. I had managed to fall back to sleep after Tim, my ex-husband, had called me about Charmaine. I looked at the clock and saw that it was a little after eight at night. I called out to my son, "Tim Jr. come here."

"Where's Max?"

"He still isn't in from work yet Ma, are you ready to get up now? I'll go get Maxine ready." He said referring to my one year old daughter.

"Ok give me a minute and we're going to make our way over to your Uncle Troy's. Your cousins are in town." I reached for my cell and dialed Max's number.

"Hey baby, I see you're up now."

"Yeah thank you for coming home in the middle of the day to check on me. I know you were busy to do that."

"Baby, I will do anything for you. I will head home in half an hour, OK?" Maxwell replied.

"Meet me at Troy's. Nitrah and the kids should be there and Troy said he was cooking. So I am getting TJ and Maxine ready to go."

"OK, look for me to be there around nine thirty. Love you babe."

"Love you too." I clicked my phone shut and rolled over out of bed.

ðð

TJ ran up to Troy's door and to ring the doorbell while I unbuckled Maxine from her car seat. I hear him yell out and jump into a man's arms. Squinting my eyes I see his tall, dark silhouette. Just as handsome as he wanted to be, Tim makes his way out to me and Maxine after telling TJ to go inside.

"Well hello my lady." Tim says planting a sloppy kiss on my cheek and then on Maxine's forehead. He lifts her up out of my hands and gives her a twirl. I admit I couldn't stand Tim and his lying cheating ass, but I tolerated him because of our son together. But this being extra mushy to my one year old daughter with my now husband Maxwell creeped me out.

"Tim stop with all of the dramatics. And I hope you don't have one of your tricks in there with you. I don't have time to be knocking a chick upside her hand because she feel like she got a place in your heart." I slammed my door shut and proceeded to walk towards Troy's door.

Tim laughed and said, "Baby you jealous. Come give me a kiss. I'll make it all better." I nudged his pretty little face out of mine and gave him the evil eye. He smirked and added, "No tricks tonight, it's just me."

"Bring my child and come on." I said walking off and rolling my eyes.

I walked through the doors with Tim mere steps away from me and the spices that Troy was cooking began to dance around me. I threw my head back and allowed the scent to make its way home in my senses and hummed. Tim suddenly popped me on the ass and laughed, "Get on in there, we are in here eating."

Picking up Maxine out of his arms, I sucked my teeth at him gave him extra attitude, turned on my heels and headed for Troy's kitchen.

I wasn't at his home often. Let's be frank, I didn't have a reason to be here unless the guys were here and I was dropping TJ off. I first saw Robert nose deep in his plate. I placed Maxine down on the couch next to TJ who was now engulfed in a video game. I walked behind Robert and planted a quick kiss to his cheek. He turned around and laughed.

"Never mess with a man when he's eating."

I nudged his head, "Whatever boy." I fell into his arms and gave him the biggest bear hug and heard Tim make a statement that he didn't get any loving from me. I ignored his comments and raced over to where I saw Nitrah's kids sitting and eating. I hugged each of them as tight as I could and gave them multiple kisses. "You guys have gotten so big."

I turned on my heels to see Troy behind me. I hadn't seen him in a few weeks since the last time I dropped TJ off with him and the boys. I walked over to him and gave him a hug. He hugged me back and said, "Nitrah is upstairs in the guest room."

I gave him a weak smile and made my way towards the stairs. It was quiet and dark up here, the complete opposite to down stairs as I crept to the guest room. I knocked lightly and pushed open the door. She laid across the bed on her back staring at the ceiling.

"Can you believe I am a guest in Troy's wife's house?" She gave a light chuckle as I walked in and sat next to her on the bed. I breathed out in relief. I was happy to see my friend, but sad at the same time.

"You were just coming for a visit and now you are here because of this," I managed to say. I fell backwards too now and laid identical to Nitrah as I stared at the ceiling.

She reached over and grabbed my hand, "It's good to see you friend."

I squeezed her hand back and said, "It's good to see you too."

Chapter 17

Troy

The house was peaceful and it was well after midnight when I stepped out of my steam shower and wrapped a towel around my waist. I walked to the sink and glanced at my phone that was flashing. I had received a text message from my wife, Gabrielle. She was flying in from Tulsa in two days. I hadn't told her we had a house full of company just yet so I was glad her job as a stylist had taken her out of town.

I placed my phone down after replying to her message and turned on the faucet. I splash warm water across my face before standing up and staring at the man in the mirror. Here I stood thirty-three, hair was fuller then it was in my twenties. I grew my beard out so it covered most of my face now but kept it cut close to my skin. I had aged. Time had passed. I chuckle slightly to myself.

This was one of the moments where I started to reflect on my life, the many women I had, the mistakes I made, and the ultimate decision to not be with Nitrah, the mother of my child. Gabrielle was a great second choice. I had loved her. I do love her. But each time I see Nitrah we exchange this stare. A stare that sends a message we both understand.

I dropped the towel and allowed my wet skin to be embraced by the cool air. I walked through the foyer of my master bedroom and glanced at the clock again. Everyone was gone and I hadn't seen Nitrah at all since she had first arrived hours ago.

The kids bathed and I even tucked them both in after we said our prayers. I figured Nitrah needed a break any way.

Once I felt dry enough I put on pajama bottoms and socks and walked out into the hallway. It was routine of me to walk around my house to check the windows and doors.

As I jogged down the stairs to begin my routine I heard someone in the kitchen and notice the light was on. I causally walk to the area and pushed open the kitchen door and poked my head in. I noticed Nitrah nose deep in the food I had cooked earlier and dressed in a t-shirt and boy shorts that barely covered her apple shaped ass. I raised an eyebrow and smirked, "Really?"

Her head jerked up as she looked for the source of the voice. Laughing she said, "Hey I slept and didn't eat so do forgive me but this food is about to be attacked." She turned her attention back to her plate and took another bite.

I sat on the bar stool in front of her and watched her eat in silence. I crossed my fingers over each one and just sat there. Her face was make-up free, her hair pulled back into a bun, and the kitchen light was making her smooth chocolate shoulders were beam as her top fell off of her right shoulder.

"Why are you up? Thought you would have been sleep by now." She walked over and sat on the stool next to me and continued to eat.

"I don't know. I guess having y'all here may have me a little on edge, you know after…"

"It's funny; Jazz was here for three hours and never mentioned her name."

We fell silent for a few minutes until I said, "You want to talk about Charmaine?" She shook her head no.

"I don't even know why I am tripping so hard. I hadn't spoken to her in years. She wasn't the woman I thought she was," she whispered. Her eyes were focused on her plate, but her mind was somewhere else.

"You remember the woman that she was to you, that's why. She was a good friend though Nitrah."

"Was she?" She stared at me and dared me to respond to her question, but I didn't have a response. "She was a manipulator and I don't know why and will never find out now that she's…"

She dropped her head and squeezed her eyes tight. I placed my hand on the top of her shoulder and squeezed it hard to help relieve the tension. "You don't have to talk about it now."

She opened her mouth to speak again when I heard my doorbell ring. Our eyes looked curiously at each other as she asked, "Your wife?"

I shook my head no. "It shouldn't be. Shit I hope not. I haven't told her y'all was staying."

Nitrah laughed and said, "Well in that case let me follow you as you open the door I must see her reaction." I waved my hand off at her and asked her to stay seated. Of course she refused.

I made my way out into the living and down the hall that led to the front door. Nitrah was merely steps behind trying to hide her obvious giggle that was echoing off the quiet walls of the house.

I flipped on the porch light and looked at the peephole. I titled my head in curiosity as Nitrah's voice broke my through process. "Who is it?" She asked.

I turned around and gave her a blank stare. I cleared my throat unlocking the locks on the door and placed my hand on the door knob. "You have company," I dryly replied. She leaned to the right to look around the door as I opened it and her eyes light up in shock.

"Cameron!"

"Hey babe!" He replied. He walked in past me without so much as a hello. I closed the door shut and it was then that he noticed someone was behind him. He acknowledged me with one word. "Troy!"

I wanted to ignore the shit out of him, but felt this wasn't the time to act like we did back in the day as college jocks. "Cameron." Yeah I knew him from the university. He was a star on University of Texas's football team. One of my rivals. How ironic. He had left years ago for Howard University right before graduation for whatever reason. I knew he had dated Nitrah back then briefly. And I knew that Nitrah's ex, Denim, had run him off.

But now he was Cameron Jr.'s dad. Our kid's shared the same blood. Talk about karma was a bitch. "I'll leave you two alone." I casually said walking past Cameron and casually kissing Nitrah on the cheek good night. I didn't care for him this is true. But I could never admit out loud that I didn't care for him for one reason only. He was with Nitrah and I wasn't.

Chapter 18

Dahlia

"Glad that's over," Joyclyn said plopping down on my bed and tossing her shoes across the room.

I rolled my eyes and watched her maneuver around what used to be my room as a teenager. "Where's your son, Darius, and why aren't you with him instead of here with me?"

"I am keeping your ass company and this is what I get? Darius is with his daddy because a growing boy needs to be with his daddy. And you and I are about to go out. Mama's wedding is over. It's been a couple days sense you found about Charmaine and you need to relax."

I threw my head back on my pillow and declined the offer. "I just want to order some Taco Casa and call it a night."

Joyclyn walked over and pulled at my arm, "Nope that is not going to happen. I know just the place to make you get out of this rut." She gave me a mysterious smile like she had a plan mapped out and was about to play Indiana Jones.

"Don't try to fix me up with some of your castoffs. You ain't too far from the days when you were Jo the Hoe."

Joyclyn laughed while throwing a dress at me, "My heydays huh? Put that dress on and bring your ass. It's time to go have some fun. Like back in the day fun."

I reluctantly did what I was told. I fixed my hair as good as I could and hopped behind the passenger seat of her car. I blew out hot air because I knew I was about to be summoned to her quest to get her groove back at my expense.

Chapter 19

Jazzaray

Maxwell was taller than me by a few inches; his strong demeanor was dominating the room. He bit his bottom lip as he propositioned me to come into his embrace and of course I did. After all these years just a simple touch from this man made me moist on cue. And he knew it too. Shoot sometimes I had to carry wipes in my purse for emergency clean ups if you know what I mean.

I had married the man of my dreams and for the first time in years my life was drama free. Well that is an occasional annoying encounter with Tim. Max grinds his hips into me and whispers, "Babe if you keep looking this good, we are going to have to ditch your friends."

I buried my face into his chest and laugh as I tried to hide my obvious grin. The DJ took us back as he began to play Bell Biv Devoe's classic "Smile Again". I whisper back, "Don't tempt me." The slow melodic rhythm from the base of the music had me in a trance. Maxwell and I grooved to the music as if we were the only ones on the dance floor. He trailed his hands up and down my back and I squeezed my pelvis tight and moaned. We hugged each other tight. Damn I loved this man.

I took a moment to stop breathing in his Giorgio Armani and tilted my head upwards. Maxwell brought his hands up to my head and brushed them across my loose curls. Then he grabbed a hand full of my hair and pulled my head backwards. He brought his lips to mine and kissed me as if it were the first time. He invaded my mouth with the warmth of his tongue and I accepted it with a strong suck of my lips.

"Ugh, like really?" Our trance was cut short as I heard Nitrah walk up behind me. "You two really do need to get a room. The hostess just buzzed us for our table so bring your ass." She walked off with Cameron trailing behind her by mere inches. My eyes turned back towards Maxell as he winked. I winked back and mouthed the words later.

It had been years but we were here at Rhapsody together. It was our favorite club from back in the day. It had expanded a little because the dance floor was larger, but it was still our Rhapsody. It felt good being back. Maxwell pulled out my chair as I took a seat. With us were Nitrah and Cameron, Nitrah's sister Tierra and her husband, Troy, Tim with his date, and Robert and his wife.

With glasses of wine already placed on the table, I took a huge gulp of its contents and exhaled. Maxwell leaned into my and whispered, "Are you ok babe?"

I gave him the 'are you seriously asking me that' look and replied, "Tim is here, what do you think?" He gave me a reassuring look as Tim called out that he wanted to make a toast.

"I am happy to see everyone, including you too Maxwell." He grinned and took a swallow of his brown liquor. His date gave an embarrassed look as I focused my attention on Nitrah, who was seated across from me. I ignored Tim's toast all together.

Call me crazy but my girl looked comfortable sitting between her new man Cameron and her old man Troy. "Y'all are looking good."

Cameron grabbed Nitrah's hand and kissed the back of it. "I haven't seen you in forever Jazz, so how have you and Maxwell been?"

I went on to tell him how I opened a second book store and that Maxwell owns and operates three restaurants. When I opened my mouth to talk about the kids, a familiar voice stopped me in my tracks.

"Well, well, well why wasn't I invited?" I turned my head and my mouth dropped in shock. Never in a million years would I think that she would show up at this very moment.

The table grew quiet. No one looked at each other they just stared at her for what seemed like an eternity. Then with a whisper of her name Nitrah called out a simple, "Hello Dahlia."

Chapter 20

Nitrah

I hadn't looked into her face in over four years. I would be lying if I didn't say this girl was like my rib. We were joined at the hip in college. She was my best friend. I thought I knew her. Cameron placed his hand on top of mine and squeezed it hard. He remembered Dahlia from back in college. It had been a decade since he had seen her, but he knew what had happened between us. He knew that after Troy and I had a child, she proceeded to fuck him.

Dahlia noticed Cameron's hand on top of mine and zoomed in on him. With squinted eyes I could tell she was trying to recall his face, his name, and where he had come from. I was on the edge of my seat prepping to tell her to get the hell away from our table.

"Cameron the football jock. Well hey now it's been a long time." She reached out to shake his hand. Being the gentlemen that he was, Cameron shook her hand back.

"Hey Dahlia." He casually said.

She smirked and said, "Oh so you remember me or perhaps the stories that have been told about me?"

He replied, "A little of both. What brings you over here?" Nobody at the table was breathing as Cameron began his questioning. The table was quiet and all eyes were roaming around the table as everyone was taking in each other's reaction.

"I'm sure you all know, I can imagine that's why you are all here together. For Charmaine." She looked over Cameron and at me. "Hello Nitrah."

I turned my head back towards her and suddenly felt Troy's hand land on my shoulder. I guess he knew me all too well. It was a sign to calm down because I was getting antsy. So I didn't reply to her hello I just stared at her. I hadn't had so much as a conversation with her since finding out she pursued Troy. It took me a year to even talk to Troy about topics outside of our child. I had healed, but now seeing her I was only hiding my pain.

Jazz rose up from her seat. She looked at me and then at Dahlia. "Ladies." She signaled with her head to follow her. I knew I didn't want to. I looked at Troy before getting out of my seat as Dahlia walked off to follow Jazz. My eyes were pierced with angry tears.

"I'm good Troy you can let me go now." He reluctantly did as I maneuvered from out of my seat and around the table. Cameron grabbed my hand and kissed it as I walked by.

My knees were weak as I tried myself to calm down and to let go of my emotions. I followed Jazz and Dahlia up the stairs. But I made sure to stay several feet away from Dahlia as I was tempted to pull her backwards by her hair.

74

Eerily she looked exactly the same, but maybe ten pounds heavier. She wore her hair shoulder length with streaks of blonde. She looked good, that I could give her.

Jazz stopped as we made our way to the upstairs balcony that overlooked downtown Dallas. Turning on her heels, her eyes landed on Dahlia, "Nice to see that you are living and breathing. I didn't think it was appropriate to have any conversation with you at that table."

"I agree," I butted in.

Dahlia's eyes shifted from me to Jazz and then back again, "That's it. Not so much as a hello. Do you ladies remember I wasn't always all bad? Hell, I am more like you then you think. We all did shit for love."

I shifted my weight from one foot to the other and rolled my eyes, "Did I fuck any of your exes?" I blurted.

Dahlia gave a slight laugh and said, "Yes, Troy!" She had me on that one.

"Dahlia now you know good and well I didn't know you and Troy dated seriously like that. You know why? Because you lied to each and every one of us and told us it was a fling. You sought me out to help you get revenge on him remember?"

Jazz rose up her hands and said, "I refuse to take it back ten years ago. What's done is done and Dahlia to be honest ain't no going back. It's been years and we only hear from you because of..." Jazz's voice trailed off.

It suddenly hit me right then and there and I wondered why no one had spoken of the obvious. The main reason why we are all here faced with the past anyway. We all routinely began to look off in different directions. It was the plague and we all knew it. It was hard to even say her name.

"I can't admit it to myself that for years we hadn't spoken and for years I forced her out of my head and now this. You know what? All this shit we went through over the years is not worth it. What if it was me, or Jazz, or damn maybe even you Dahlia? What If it was one of us and we died without so much as I am sorry?" I managed to say without breaking into tears.

Jazz leaned backwards on a railing and folded her arms across her chest. "Are you asking for a truce?"

Dahlia added, "Right here?" She curiously raised an eyebrow.

I waved them both off. "Now wouldn't be right, later. Later Dahlia. I can't deal right now. Just give me your number and we can all sit down and talk another time." I eyed her and added, "Don't get it twisted. I don't like you, but I know if Charmaine was here this is what she would have wanted."

She pulled out her cell and I had her text my phone. I would be lying if I said I wasn't too excited about seeing her again but life was short and for Charmaine it ended at the age of thirty-two.

Chapter 21

Troy

I listened to my daughter Nina go on and on about this boy at school whom she claimed she couldn't stand but I was sure she had a little crush going on. At the same time I looked over to see Cameron Jr. playing on my game system.

"You works my nerves on purpose Daddy." Nina added. I eyed her and curiously laughed. I wasn't used to this and I couldn't imagine how Nitrah was dealing with this on a regular basis.

"Baby girl, you seem to be talking about this boy who is hundreds of miles away quite a lot. You think perhaps you want to talk about something else?"

I had to look twice at her when I noticed she rolled her eyes and added, "Ugh Daddy I swear I can't have girl talk with you. I'm going to my room to call my friend." My mouth was half way open prepping to say something, but I was more shocked all at the same time.

I jumped out of my seat and search for Nitrah whom I last saw going out to my patio. I found her seated on the edge of the steps with a glass of wine in her right hand. Her head was looking upward towards the sky. She in deep thought. I cleared my throat so that she knew I was standing behind her.

I didn't look back as she whispered, "It's quiet back here. Does it ever freak you out that where ever you are in the world everyone is looking at the same moon?"

I didn't answer as I wasn't sure if it was a question she wanted an answer to. I sat down next to her. My hip to her hip, we sat as if we were connected. "I come out here a lot too. To think of the next play for my next football game I'm coaching, to talk to Nina on the phone as she goes on and on about everything, or just to think."

She laughed and pointed at a brick I had placed behind my patio table. "Yeah I found your stash."

I jerked my head back and laughed, "You found my stash here?"

"Brown liquor and Kush huh? Does the university know their coach blazes it up at night?" She laughed out.

I got up and went over to where I hide my weed and Crown liquor. I pulled out a cigar and turned towards her and held up my goodies. Gabrielle had no idea about the little fun fest I had in my back yard often. "Perfect time to go ahead and get relaxed. Where did your boy go?" I asked as I sat back down next to her and opened up the cigar and dumped its contents to fill it with the weed.

"Cameron went to go see his mother. He'll probably stay over tonight. He hasn't seen her in a while."

"And he didn't mind you staying here with me?"

"Does Gabrielle?" She shot back.

I laughed and said, "She will once she pulls up."

Nitrah jerked her head at me and said, "You haven't told her yet? This is going to be hilarious. You know she doesn't like me or the fact that Cameron Jr. calls you Pops."

I added, "I don't think Cameron enjoys that either, but it's not like I give a fuck." I began to lick one the cigar to roll it up tight. I took a lighter and trailed it across the cigar.

Nitrah whispered, "Maybe I should just marry him and call it a day. He's asked a couple times."

I stopped midstride in my quest to get my weed the way I wanted and stared at her, "Married." I didn't know how I felt about that, but I couldn't let it show on my face.

"Yeah the same thing you did two years ago. Move on."

I shot back, "Ideal thing to do once you had a child with someone else five years ago." She stared at me as if she were offended that I had said what I said. I looked away and began to light up my weed and took a long drag of its contents. I didn't want to look her in the face. It was obvious we both held animosity towards each other.

Nitrah reached over and took the smoke in between her index and thumb and brought it to her lips. I watched her every move as her chest caved in when she took a long puff and held her breath. She closed her mouth tightly and took a deep breath out and the smoke began to escape her body through her nose. I watched in amazement as she opened her mouth, dropped her head back, and allowed the smoke to then escape though her mouth.

She took one more puff before handing it back to me. "Oh really?" I asked curiously. I didn't know she could smoke weed like that, or at all for that matter.

"I will do just about anything tonight after seeing Dahlia tonight," she whispered. Her focus was straight forward staring the night's darkness in the eye. I could read her expression, but took another puff and passed it back to her.

I took my hand and pulled pieces of hair from her face and wrapped it behind her ear. Her face full was of mixed emotions. "I know it wasn't your intention to be here for this."

"You ever feel like life dealt you a hand you wanted to throw back in and get another deal? As if you were playing a hand of spades and wanted to cut books to get the win? I have been feeling like that ever since I was told Charmaine was dead. She didn't know my kids; she didn't know me for years now. And we made it that way. We had an unforgiving heart and now I can't take it back."

"If she was here, would you take it back? Would you forgive her?" I asked smoking the last of the cigar's contents.

Nitrah grew quiet before answering me. Turning her head she looked me straight in the face and said, "I would have said I forgive you for hurting Jazz like she did, for being a person I didn't know. But I know we wouldn't have had a relationship."

"But you forgave me. You are sitting here with me now."

80

She sucked her teeth and waved me off her hand and said, "That's different."

"How is that different?"

"You're Troy, you're family. I…"

"You what?"

Again silence. Nitrah confusingly looked at me and squint her eyes in confusion. "You know Troy."

I dropped the butt of the cigar into the grass and blew the remainder of the smoke through my mouth and then turned my attention back to Nitrah. "Yeah I know; it's something I knew even as you carried that man's child. You know and I know."

"You knew it as you watched Gabrielle walk down that aisle and then said I do to her too." She blurted out with a hint of anger in her voice.

I leaned in closer to her. Inch by inch I brought my being closer to hers. It wasn't that I desperately wanted to hear something that I already knew. I wasn't on a quest to get her to do something that I was daring her to admit. I suddenly felt the urge to be closer. I want to be closer to her and to feel her breath on my skin. Nitrah raised her hand and stopped me in midstride and said, "You chose her, not me. I chose him, not you."

"Was that a mistake or is that how you want it?" I whispered back. My lips were mere inches away from hers. I was so close that I could see her beating heart rise and fall though her shirt. I could feel the heat from her skin dance across my flesh.

"Troy..." I heard her say. Nitrah suddenly jumped back as my vision was clearer. There was a new light that was beaming on us as I heard my name again. "Troy!"

I heard my name but Nitrah's mouth wasn't moving. I jumped out of my trance as confusion began to take over. I turned my head back towards the light and jumped up and shock. "Gabrielle, baby!"

My wife was home in just the nick of time.

Chapter 22

Nitrah

I told Cameron Jr. and Nina to get in the bed and grabbed my keys and headed for the front door. I watched my kids storm their way up the stairs and then called out to them, "Go grab a night cap and let's go."

Troy rushed over to me after leaving Gabrielle standing in the middle of the living room and asked, "What are you doing?"

"I'm taking them to their grandmothers. My sisters are there and I could use some girl time."

"Are you leaving because of Gabrielle? She'll understand."

I eyed him and whispered, "She caught us nose deep in each other's faces. Go handle your wife Troy and for once just let me go do me." I jogged up the stairs to go grab some clothes but not before saying, "Gabrielle it is nice to see you. Glad you made it back in town safely."

She folded her hands across her chest and just gave me a head nod. I ignored the gesture and continue my stride up the stairs. I could hear her yelling even before I made it into my guest room. I grabbed some shoes, panties, and a change of clothes and threw them into one of my oversized purses and rushed over to the other guest room the kids were sharing.

"Let's go."

"Gabrielle doesn't want us here?" Nina asked being nosey. I assured her that Gabrielle was fine but their grandmother wanted them to come over and to hurry up. As we jogged down the stairs I noticed that Troy and Gabrielle had moved their heated conversation into their bedroom. I grabbed the knob of the front door and order the kids to rush to the car.

I shut the door and headed to my car. I was almost there when I heard the front door opening. I ran towards my car and opened the door. Troy called out my name. I waved him off and said I would call later. But I knew my next mission was to sneak back over and get the rest of our things. I didn't need the drama or the obvious unanswered emotions from both Troy and I. I put my car in drive and pulled out of his driveway like a thief who made off with a gold mine.

ðð

Mama opened the door and hugged us all one by one. She gave the kids hugs and kisses on their cheeks and I saw them slyly trying to wipe off the saliva Mama left behind. I found Tierra and Raven my old room lying across the bed. I barged in dropped my bag by the door.

Raven looked at me up and down as Tierra began to laugh, "Ummm I am guessing Gabrielle Washington is back in town."

"Dang, I owe you twenty dollars." Tierra said to Raven as she got up, grabbed her purse, and pulled out the money.

"Ha, ha, ha, not funny. And yes she is home and she didn't waste any time getting in Troy's ass."

Tierra plopped back down on the bed and muted the TV and said, "That's because ole Troy still want your kitty kat." They began to laugh out loud as I started to shush them.

"I don't want the kids to hear y'all.' I added.

"Girl please. They're in there playing with their cousins. Even grown ass Nina ain't listening to us right now."

I plopped down on the floor and buried my face in my hands, "I think he was going to kiss me tonight and Gabrielle saw it."

Raven blurted out, "You're lying? I don't believe this."

Tierra's head fell back in laughter, "Oh I can see it, that man ain't ever stopped loving you. I told you two years ago he was marrying her because you were with Cameron, had a child with Cameron, and moved to Houston to be with Cameron. Need I say any more?"

"It's was too much baggage with him, still is, and ten years later we still have this merry go round."

"Well then chick stop going in circles and find your straight line and walk that, shoot. Because truth be told, you two are both getting on my nerves." Raven said stuffing her face with popcorn.

"The man is married now and Nitrah might as well be married too. I say leave it alone," Tierra added.

"You two aren't helping me." I poked my lip out to resemble a big kid.

85

"No trick you just want us to say go ahead girl, break up his marriage, break Cameron's heart, and have your blended family" Raven mocked.

"Well damn Raven, tell me how you really feel?" I pulled out my cell phone to text Cameron and noticed a text from Troy. It read to meet him at the French Lake.

I text back I am not doing this again. I cut my phone off without waiting from a response from Cameron or Troy. I turned my attention back to Raven, who was eyeing me.

"Was that Troy?"

I raised my phone up to show her that I turned it off, "If it was I ain't talking to him tonight." I crawled over on my knees and grabbed some of their popcorn and added, "Turn the movie back on. I need a carefree night tonight."

Tierra unmuted the TV and then began to sniff the air and eyeballed me, "Chick do you know you smell just like weed?" I eyed both of them and we all burst out in laughter. This is what I needed. A night with my sisters to just be me.

Chapter 23

Dahlia

I had the TV and the light on in my hotel room but I wasn't watching anything. I wasn't interested in what was on TV; I wasn't interested in talking to anyone on the phone. My mind was rewinding my encounter with my former friends, my former family. Then it began to get stuck on seeing Robert again and Troy. Damn I had a lot of skeletons at that table. No wonder I was no longer in that circle. I had cut each and every one of the people who at some point cared about me. I had to be honest with myself. It made me sick to my stomach.

I walked over to my cash bar, popped open a vodka and downed its contents. I flinched and coughed as the strong liquid made its way down my throat. I followed the alcohol with a glass of water.

I picked up my phone and searched for any missed calls. None. I searched through my texts and saw the last one was from Nitrah stating she had my number. I dropped the phone back on the bed and fell backwards with my arms and legs extended eagle style. I was bored. I was lonely. I had no friends. I hadn't had any in a while as I'd thrown myself into my work over the past few years.

It didn't faze me for a while that my life had gone a totally different direction. But now being back here was bringing up all those old feelings. The times when I used to smile just because. I jumped up at the knock on my door and frowned as I looked at the clock. It was late.

I tiptoed over to the door and peeked through the peep hole. I blew out a sigh of relief and place my hand on the door knob as I opened the door. I greeted, "Heifer!"

She smirked and passed me with a greeting, "Slut!" Dropping her bags down on my hotel room floor she began to kick off her shoes. I closed the door and followed behind her.

"Monica did you not get your own room?"

"Nope, I figured I would just mooch off of you for the night." She looked around my suite as if she was inspecting it and giving it her approval. She stopped before the opened patio door and walked out. The view overlooked downtown Fort Worth.

"I expected you here yesterday to be honest. Why the delay?"

She turned to face me and pressed her back up against the railing and folded her arms across her chest. "I went to North Carolina yesterday. I wanted to speak to the detective on the case."

I raised a curious eyebrow and asked, "And what did he say."

"What we already knew. She was dead for at least three weeks, strangled. He didn't want to say it, but I know that she suffered. She didn't die quickly."

I slouched down on the bed and dropped my head. I threw my hand up at her in hopes that she got the idea that I couldn't hear anymore.

With tears in my eyes I looked back at her and asked, "When will her body be here?"

She looked me dead in the eyes, without so much as a blink. He face was blank and lacked any emotion. I would be lying if I said I didn't feel a little uneasy, but I did. Monica was always a mystery to me. Her and Charmaine's past never made sense to me either. But I never asked.

"Two days. We have two days Dahlia."

Chapter 24

Nitrah

The morning's sunrise was finally making its way over the clouds. I was already on my second cup of coffee as I sat on Mama's porch. Everyone was still asleep. I knew the kids would be knocked out because they didn't fall asleep until well after three in the morning.

I turned as I heard the front door open and out came my Mama's head as she poked it through the screen door, "Gonna make ya some some girts and eggs. You want that this morning?"

I smiled and began to beam with excitement, "Yes ma'am can you add some of Granny's homemade biscuits too?" I gave her a childish plea as I blinked my eyes more than necessary.

She waved her hand off at me and reassured me that she could handle making a big breakfast for us this morning. I hurriedly turned my phone on to tell Cameron to bring himself over to get some of Mama's food. I hadn't turned it on since last night. As soon as the screen lit up my phone buzzed back to back from texts and voicemail alerts.

I saw several from Troy. I rolled my eyes. A reply from Dahlia saying ok. I rolled my eyes. One from Jazz saying 'goodnight' so I texted her 'good morning'. A few from Cameron that I skimmed through. And then my finger stopped on an all too familiar name. I smiled wide. My stomach began to flutter.

His text read, "Raven told me you are in town. I know you get your ass up early so I'll see you around eight in the morning."

My eyes jolted to the clock that read 7:47 am. I hurried jumped up off of Mama's steps and rushed into the house. With one hand I tore off my head rag and the other I began to aggressively wipe my eyes. I search in my bag for some shorts and a t-shirt. I rushed in the bathroom began to wash my face and brush my teeth.

Pulling the rollers out of my head as well I ran my fingers through the curls and applied lotion on my face. I felt I was satisfied with my look as I glanced at myself through the mirror. I looked cute enough for it to be morning, but not obvious for him to know I was trying to look cute. But knowing him, he would know my efforts. I laughed at myself at the thought of seeing him.

It was going to be a surreal moment. I walked back towards the kitchen to find Mama focused on beating a bowl of eggs. "Did you add that Cajun seasoning you used to use?"

She didn't take her focus off of the bowl of eggs as she called out, "Stop being nosey and cut the station on Heaven 97." I got up and turned on Mama's old stereo system to 970 am. The oldest gospel station in Fort Worth. I bent down and gave a heavy blow on the dusty system that was probably as old as me. The cassette player dispenser's door wouldn't even close properly. The dust was flying everywhere as I it away from my face.

"Mama why don't you get a new radio? I'll go with you today and we can pick one out at Best Buy."

She gave me the blankest stare that I was sure could kill me on spot. "And who is going to operate it once you're gone? Plus that radio works just fine. Your brother picked it out when he was two. My good luck charm." She gave a hearty laugh as I decided not to fight to losing battle.

"You need some help?"

"Child gone somewhere. You come here once a blue moon and want to cook in my kitchen. Get!" She waved a kitchen towel at me as I skipped towards the front door in laughter. I was glad not to cook anyway.

Opening the door I walk back out and take a seat on the steps and pull out my cell phone from my pocket. Pulling my hair behind my left ear I click on messages and scroll down. Suddenly a message popped up, Here!

I looked across the street and saw a black Mustang. I smiled widely. I knew it had to have been him pulling up in a car like that. I stood up and called out to the car. Nothing. I looked down at my phone to see if there was another message. Nothing. I took a couple steps down on the ground now and starred at the car that had to have been all but thirty feet away.

The door flew open without so much as a warning and he quickly stepped out. He had gained weight not in a bad way. He stood taller in my opinion, towering over my 5'7" foot fame, his dark smooth face was now covered in a full beard, his hair cut low but curly. He was dressed in jeans and a white tee, his silver Cartier watch blinded me as it reflected off the sun.

I was beaming, I was excited. I kicked off my sandals and ran bare foot across Mama's lawn. I screamed out, "Denim!"

He held out his arms and allowed me to jump up into them. I wrapped my legs around his waist, my arms draped around his neck as I squeezed tightly. He laughed as and kissed my forehead as I planted a wet kiss on his cheek. Leaning backwards as if I was a small child in his arms I whispered, "I am so happy to see you."

He took a deep breath and smiled lightly and said, "Nitrah it's been a long time."

Chapter 25

Troy

I followed in behind Tim who arrogantly waltzed into the Lyrical Lounge. He was in search of his next girl or victim as I liked to call it. I constantly tell him to stop trying to work Jazz's nerves. One day Maxwell was going to beat the shit out of him. But, the more I told him to back up the more he pressed forward.

I walked in and sat at the bar. I hadn't seen Nitrah since she rushed out of my house once Gabrielle caught us about to do what we both know what was about to go down. I couldn't halfway believe it myself. I thought that chapter was closed. And I thought I was done being that guy. The one who jumped from one woman to another.

I asked the bartender to get me a Crown and Coke. Tim walked up behind me and gave me a brotherly pat on the back, "You alright bro, ordering your Crown at noon?"

I glanced at the clock and noticed the time. "I didn't realize it was early, but yeah. Need a drink right now."

"Anything you want to talk about?" He asked as he ordered a plate of wings.

"Nope. I'm good." I managed to say after taking a swallow of the drink's contents. "You need to worry about Maxwell getting on that ass if you don't stop messing with Jazz and taunting her with that child play shit."

"I just be playing with her. I don't give a fuck how long she been married to that nigga. She was married to me first which means she will always be Mrs. Meadows."

I waved him off, "Arrogant ass fool. Don't ask me to jump in once Maxwell start..." He cut me off.

"What about Gabrielle? She may be pretty and half Latino, but those are the chicks that add shit to your food and kill your ass. Don't fuck with her man. I saw how you were looking at Nitrah. You are always looking at that chick like that every time she comes into town."

I waved him off, "She'll be fine."

I felt a hand on my back and turned. "Hey Jazz." I leaned in and gave her a hug. Tim jumped up and gestured that he wanted a hug as well. Jazz declined. I burst into laughter.

"Jazz stop doing me like that." Tim whined acting as if he was heartbroken.

Jazz looked over to Tim and asked, "I just left the book store next door for a couple hours, but you still have to get Tim Jr. this evening from basketball practice. And don't have one of your sluts in the car." When she pointed her finger in his face he pretended to jerk forward and bite it. Jazz jumped back.

I called out, "Yo dog stop." I had a serious tone. The game playing with her had to stop.

He laughed it off and ordered himself a drink. "It's about to go down you know." Jazz said sitting down on the stool next to me and whisking around in her chair. She eyed the front door.

I took a hard swallow of my drink and slammed the empty glass back on the counter. I asked the bar tender for another one. Jazz eyed me and said, "Keep your cool Mr. Washington. It's only Nitrah's first love and your ex." She winked and turned her attention to the door.

With one hard swing the door opened and Nitrah took a step in. Since she was the owner, I knew the Lyrical Lounge would be the first place she would come to today. She liked to spend most of her time here when she was in town.

I cringed at the sight of his hands on her waist as he followed in. Jazz hopped up and ran over to him wrapping her arms around his tall frame. I stood up and faced the man I had fought neck and neck with over Nitrah years ago. I extended my hand, "Denim!"

He gave a slick smile, rubbed his beard with one hand in an attempt to look as if he was trying to remember who I was. I wanted to punch him dead in his face, but as tall as he had gotten I would land at his neck. "Man I am just playing. What up Troy?" Denim laughed and gave me a one hand pound and embrace. I gave a light chuckle and let that awkward moment pass.

"The kids didn't come with you?" I asked eyeing Nitrah.

She walked past me and immediately jumped into the trance of operating a business. She was behind the counter in a matter of seconds checking on everything. "No, they are at Mama's with their cousins. Cameron is going to pick them up and take them over his Mom's house.

"My daughter?" I asked.

Everyone began to spread to the outside patio once they knew a debate of our kids was about to commence. "Ummm yeah our daughter. What's the problem?"

"Why is Cameron taking my daughter to go see his family when I haven't even taken her to go see mine?"

Nitrah shrugged her shoulders and laughed, "Well I figured you were over there playing house with Mrs. La Caliente. I heard Tim laugh out as he headed outside with his plate of wings. I ignored his snickers and stomped over to the counter where Nitrah stood.

"Look Troy you want to go pick up Nina go right ahead. Make sure you tell her why she can't go see her Nana who turns 92 next month."

I pointed my finger at her and yelled out, "There you go again. That ain't her family. I am. I feel like you trying to make this Cameron nigga her daddy. Bad enough he lives with my child, but now he gets priority too."

Nitrah rolled her eyes and blew air through her mouth as if she were annoyed. I studied her expression. She was agitated at this conversation. Hell so was I. It wasn't like I wanted to have this conversation, especially in front of Denim. I could never stand the sight of him. I ignored the obvious stares from the crew and was thankful that Jazz was shooing all of them outside so that we could have some privacy.

Chapter 26

Nitrah

Turning on my heels I asked the bartender to go restock the bar as I made my way into the back storage room. When I wasn't in town I had my manager take over everything. But when I was here I took control of things.

I could hear Troy behind me tussling around the bar area to follow me to the back. I increased the speed in my steps to dodge his efforts of catching up to me. "Don't follow me!" I announced pulling the storage room door open and flicking on the light.

Troy rushed in behind me gripping my arm in the process. I swung around in anger preparing to slap the shit out of him. Pushing me in, he kicked the door behind him with his foot and pulled me into him. His breathing was so heavy that I could feel the rise and fall of his chest. His eyes were filled with anger, tension, and then I saw that familiar stare. Passion.

I turned my face away from his cutting off our eye contact and whined the words, no! Pulling myself away from him I felt the weakness in my efforts to escape. Was I trying to get away or did I really want him to force me to look back into his eyes. Could I possibly play with the idea of allowing this man back into my space again, into my heart, and into my life? It had been years, but something was different this time. This time I felt a sense of urgency.

With his left hand he reached for my chin and turned my head back towards him. I first snatched my face out of his hand and he quickly gripped my chin again forcing me to look at him. He pushed me backwards against the wall and whispered my name, "Nitrah!"

I whined again this time begging him to not go there. I knew what he was doing. I knew good and well what was about to happen and I was fighting him. Trust me that I was. I wasn't his anymore and he wasn't mine. I stood there in the audience and watched him marry someone else. I watched him say I do to her, not me. So why am I here again? Why am I yet again fighting the urgency to feel him inside of me?

I felt the temperature of my body increase to a dangerous level. The room was beginning to get so hot that sweat beads were forming at the crown of my head. I yanked my arm out of his hand and pushed him backwards on his chest just as I felt a sudden wind of chills attack my knees. I began to crumble under as Troy caught me with the slip of his hand.

As he pulled me upwards our breathing was in sync. My lower lip dropped open in hopes of gasping for more air. I could barely breathe. I grew enough courage to stare at him again. My eyes met his as we stood there wrapped in each other's being, nose to nose, eye to eye; my soul was in adjacent to his.

"I love you so much." Troy said planting his forehead onto mines. I blinked slowly and took a big swallow in an effort to bring moisture to my mouth.

I shook my head no as I mustered up the courage just to say his name, "Troy!"

He stopped me midsentence as he hungrily took my mouth into his. He grabbed the back of my head, took a handful of hair, and pushed me further into his mouth. I opened my mouth and allowed his tongue to invade it. I couldn't fight the desire that was boiling through my veins. My mind ran rapid as I realized that I was kissing the man I had vowed to let go. But should I?

Troy pushed me upward and threw my body into his arms wrapping my very being around his. I gripped his body tightly as I held on for dear life. I didn't bother to resist as I felt his hands trail down my thighs and in between my legs. He searched his way through and pushed my panties to the side. Jamming his fingers inside of me I gasped for air. I felt my panties become drenched in my desire for him.

Reaching down I played with the opening of his pants long enough to hear them drop at his ankles. With one swift move he pulled himself out and found the opening to a place we had long ago visited. In one hard thrust he was inside of me. I squeezed my pelvis as tightly as I could to tackle the erotic rush that suddenly was taking me to my peak. He pushed himself in and out of me. What lasted for only minutes felt like hours.

With his right hand he covers my mouth pushing my head backwards onto the wall. My eyes rolled upward as I stared at the flickering light on the ceiling. My muffled moans could only be heard within these four walls as I felt myself began to limp over with satisfaction. Because of our sudden desire for each other didn't take much of an effort for either of us to reach that orgasmic high. Troy slipped out of me and allowed his seeds to fall into his hand.

My feet hit the floor. Both of our breathing was so erratic it took up most of the oxygen in the room. I zoomed in on a paper towel rack and went to retrieve some. I had to quickly wipe away our indiscretion before anyone else had a chance to realize our faults.

Chapter 27

Jazzaray

I sat down next to Denim on the patio of the Lyrical Lounge and I couldn't help the fact that I was beaming all over. "It has been years. I feel like you abandoned your family here in Fort Worth Mr. Big Time Producer."

Denim nudged my shoulder and laughed. "Never that Jazz. Life has been busy shoot. I come into town often. It's just when I do it is to check on Mama and the rest of the family."

"Well you know I am about to be nosey, who are you with now? Is she cute, how many baby mamas you got? Where ya living? Come on spill the juice."

Tim butted in and said, "Damn Jazz let the man answer a question."

I waved him off and turned my attention back to Denim. He laughed before saying, "I narrowed it down to two women, no kids yet, and I live in Miami. I got a place here too you know?"

I raised an eyebrow, "Oh, so you do come here often. I saw in a magazine that you were dating a singer what's her name, Ciara."

"That was a rumor." He took a swallow of bottled water and looked off.

"Are you in town because of Charmaine?"

Denim looked at me curiously as his mouth fell open. "Damn, that's a name I haven't heard come from anyone's mouth in a few years. Nah Nitrah told me weeks ago she was going to be in town this weekend so I surprised her and met her at her mom's house this morning. What about Charmaine?"

Just as I was prepping to open my mouth to tell him what happened to her; the door opened up behind me. We all turned around simultaneously as my eyes jumped to a familiar face. I turned to Tim who had dropped his food in shock and said, "Well, well, well I guess we all return the funkytown at some point huh?

Chapter 28

Dahlia

I nudged Monica to play nice. She hadn't seen Tim in years. Not since we were sleeping with him when he was married to Jazz. I didn't want to be the source of drama either, for once. I walked over to Denim who had stood up from his chair by now and extended my hand. I was shocked to see him. It seemed everybody and their Mama was in town this week.

"Handshakes, I know it's been a while, but a brother can give you a hug now?" Denim reached in and gave me that old brotherly hug he used to give. It was weird I must admit. I hadn't seen him in forever and when I used to see him back in the day when Nitrah and I were best friends and he was dating her I couldn't stand him. Mainly because he was a hoe and always cheated on Nitrah.

"It's good to see you Denim." I turned and acknowledged Tim and then looked at Jazz. "Hey Jazz!"

She stood up from her seat placing her hands in her pockets. "Dahlia!" I wanted to roll my eyes at her obvious attitude, but thought against it. Jazz looked over my shoulder and zoomed in on Monica, "Michelle was it?" She asked.

Monica snickered slightly before waving her hand off, "No, it's Monica. How are you Jazz and Tim?" She turned her attention to Tim who was planted in his seat. It was definitely an awkward moment. Tim just nodded his head.

"It's good to see you all here but umm where is Nitrah?"

"Here, what's up?" I turned to see Nitrah and Troy walking up behind me.

"Oh hey I didn't see you when we walked in."

Troy interrupted and said, "We were in the back." I raised a curious eyebrow, but decided to not press that issue either. I was biting my tongue a lot in these last five minutes.

"I came here to see if you all wanted to ride over to Spencer's Funeral home?"

Nitrah stood next to Jazz and looked at me, "The funeral home?"

"Yeah Charmaine's body is finally here."

Denim blurted out, "Body? Wait. Someone want to tell me what's going on?"

Monica looked at him and licked her lips obviously flirting in the same process. I rolled my eyes as she opened her mouth to speak, "Yes ummm it's nice to meet you." She shook his hand. "Charmaine was killed that's why we are all here. Isn't that why you're here?"

Denim blankly stared at her and then dropped her hand. He turned his attention back to Nitrah and then eyed Tim. "Yo Tim you never told me Charmaine was dead man." We all turned our heads and looked at Tim then back at Denim.

Nitrah's weight switched from one leg to the other as she asked, "You two talk?"

It was as if Denim started to realize where he was and secretly hoped he could take back the words that just escaped his mouth. I watched his demeanor and something wasn't adding up. "No. I saw him a few weeks back when I was in town that's all."

Tim dryly responded. "She wasn't dead then."

It fell silent for what seemed like minutes until Jazz said, "Let's just go. I want to get this over with. I'll go call Maxwell to meet us."

"I'll call Cameron." Nitrah added as she and Jazz walked past me and Monica.

"I'll go call my brother." Troy said following behind them. Soon enough Denim and Tim followed them inside.

"We'll be waiting outside in the car." I yelled behind him.

Monica elbowed me and laughed, "Did you see little Ms. Jazz act as if she didn't remember my name. That bitch remembers me and my fucking her husband."

She smirked as I stopped in my tracks and pointed my finger at her, "Not today Monica, not now. And I saw how you looked at Denim. Look away from him too. I have enough lasting drama with this circle and I don't need any more grief, especially none started by you."

Monica held up hands in surrender and walked off. I rolled my eyes at the back of my head secretly wishing this week was over already.

Chapter 29

Nitrah

I found myself in the bathroom of the Spencer Funeral home. Everyone who was anyone in Fort Worth was buried by this funeral home. I personally had been in this building many times growing up as a kid. Each time I was here I hated it of course. And like most days I wasn't ready for this occasion either.

I wet a napkin cold enough to my liking and placed it on the back of my neck. Jazz walked in and eyed me. "Are you ready for this?"

"No. Is Maxwell out there yet? I'm waiting on Cameron. He had to drop the kids off."

"Yes, he is here. I am keeping him away from that jezebel Monica."

I rolled my eyes at the sound of her name, "Go figure she's here with Dahlia too." I stood there for a moment stuck in my own thoughts.

Jazz placed her hand on my shoulder, "What are you thinking about?"

My eyes grew teary. My throat grew tight as I tried to swallow my saliva. "Ten years ago we were just kids fresh out of college. Playing the love game, dating, hanging out, breaking hearts, we were just living the life. And now look. Dahlia is a stranger and Charmaine…." My voice trailed off.

Jazz placed her hand on my shoulders I looked at her and smiled, "You were just the baby. Boy weren't we a bad influence on you."

"Hey look ahere now. I got Tim Jr. out the deal and then my fine ass husband Maxwell."

I laughed and said, "Yeah, but you had to get through Tim's immature ass first. And to think we all use to think that brother was fine." I shook my head.

"Girl we thought he was fine because he is. It's his childish ass personality and the whore within him that turns us off."

I grew quiet for a moment then looked Jazz in the eyes, "Do you think we will ever be back close to Dahlia?"

"Hmm let me think. She was fucking Troy after y'all had a baby, was the reason we did that scam on Troy all those years ago, and to top that off she shows up with the trick who was fucking my husband at the time. I think not."

"I look at her and I don't understand sometimes. She isn't the same person we knew in college and then lately just looking at her, I see loneliness and a glimpse of the woman I used to know."

"Tell that to Robert. She broke his heart many of times. Glad that brother moved on too," Jazz said cutting me off. I laughed and decided not to press the issue of Dahlia and threw my wet napkin in the trash.

"Come on Jazz. Let's go see our friend."

Jazz raised an eyebrow before gripping my hand as if she could barely stand. I saw the fear and pain in her eyes and I knew why. I wanted to break down in a crying spell from just remembering the pain Jazz and I went through because of Dahlia and Charmaine.

"Nitrah pray for me please. I can't stand the fact that I hate Charmaine. I hate her for what she did, the lies she told, the secrets she kept, the fact that she was with Tim before I even was. I can't stand the betrayal. But since she is dead I can't hold on to it anymore. I need to forgive her. I need her to know that I can move past it now and not hold a grudge."

I kissed the back of Jazz's hand and squeezed it tightly. "Well then let's go tell her." As we walked out of the bathroom together I spotted Cameron walking in. Immediately I began to clinch my pearls subconsciously thinking he could smell Troy down there. I needed to clean up physically and emotionally.

Jazz and I let go of each other's hands as I walked to him and she to Maxwell. Cameron opened his arms and I fell into his embrace and started to weep. He kissed my forehead and whispered that he loved me. I did love this man. We had a child together. But I also knew that I loved Troy and as I pressed my face against Cameron's chest my eyes wandered out into the lobby and landed on Troy. As he sat there watching us his demeanor was unreadable. It was in that moment that I knew I loved him more.

Chapter 30

Tim Meadows

I sat down in the chair closest to the door and watched as everyone stood around waiting to see Charmaine's body. I couldn't deal with the mystery and I didn't want to. I hadn't spoken to Charmaine since our last argument. It had always ended in her announcing her love for me. But being the man that I was, love wasn't just in the cards for me.

I had loved once. Jazzaray. I had loved that woman. I had plotted to get her years ago, accomplished that, but the old me caused me to lose her when I took up a relationship with Monica. The funny thing is I couldn't stand the sight of Monica now and I knew her ways. I laughed at myself as I noticed that she took a liking to Denim. I could pimp a hoe like her any day I thought to myself.

But I couldn't act out of order now that Monica was in town. I wasn't surprised that she was here anyway being that she was Charmaine's oldest friend from Winston-Salem. I knew all of Charmaine's history. I guess you can say I helped groom her into the low self-esteem woman that she had become. But I would never admit that out loud.

It wasn't my fault she was damaged goods from the jump and allowed me to do anything I ever wanted to her. It was easy so don't blame me for taking up the opportunity.

Deep in my thoughts I glanced up to find Monica walking over to me. "Are you ready to see our girl? I mean you got a history with her that spans about fifteen years right?" She smirked.

I shushed her and signaled for her to take a seat next to me. "I knew you would show up here eventually and to be honest I am not happy to see you. Don't start any shit this week Monica."

"Or what? Are you going to try and tame me like you did Charmaine for years? I never understood why she loved you so much. You were a piece of shit."

"But you liked fucking this piece of shit. Look here Monica. You and I both know what's up alright. You stay in your lane and shut the hell up. Nobody needs to know about Charmaine's past."

She eyed me and smirked again, "Her past or yours?"

I stared at her as I fought the urge to slap her in her mouth. I couldn't stand a woman that talked out of turn. She would get hers for sure.

"You know one thing you never knew Tim is that Charmaine told me about the scam. How would you feel if everyone here found out that you were the brainchild behind a scam that ruined your best friend Troy's life? Lost him the love of his life?"

I tilted my head in curiosity. I didn't know for sure if Monica knew the history behind the scam for me to get with

Jazz. Which in turn caused Charmaine to convince Dahlia that it was her idea to get revenge on my boy Troy. However being as though Monica and Charmaine held such long history, I always assumed she knew anyway. So this threat she was throwing I was always prepared for.

"Monica, I promise you I am not the one to threaten. You don't want to be lying next to your friend Charmaine do you?"

She leaned back and examined me before rising up from her seat. She didn't turn around and look my way again. And to be honest that's the way I wanted it. Next thing was to get her ass back to Chicago.

Chapter 31

Troy

I slid my tongue across my teeth and squeeze my hands into a fist. I noticed Nitrah over there with Cameron. The vision itself worked my nerves. I was antsy. I was agitated. And for the life of me I couldn't stop it from annoying the shit out of me.

My heart jumped in an unsuspected rhythm as Gabrielle, Robert, and his wife walked through the door of the funeral home. I don't know why I was nervous. It wasn't like a sign that Nitrah's juices was all over my dick was on my forehead. Karma wouldn't screw me over that bad, now would it?

I gave Robert a one hand embrace, kissed his wife on the cheek, and lastly turned my attention to my wife. She smiled slightly. I imagined she was a little unsure of how I would receive her. I left the house with us in a full out fight over Nitrah this, the kids that. It was an argument we had every time they were in town.

I kissed her cheek and said, "Hey!"

"Hi. I wanted to come and support you Troyon. I
don't want to continue to fight. I know she was your friend
so I am here." Gabrielle said. I nodded my head OK.

"They haven't told us that we could go in and see her
yet." I told the three of them.

Robert's wife's eyes wondered around the room and
she suddenly grew excited. "Isn't that the famous rapper guy
Denim O?"

I turned my head and followed where her eyes had
landed and grew even more agitated. "That's Denim, Nitrah's
old friend. And he's not a rapper, he's a producer and DJ."
My tone was dry and disinterested.

"Nitrah?" She quizzed again. "Wait is Nitrah and the
kids in town? I haven't seen them?" I pointed to where she
stood and told her to go say hi. Gabrielle eyed me with so
much anger I swear her eyes were pierced with fire.

I shrugged my shoulders, "What now Gabrielle?"

Robert interjected, "Y'all cool?"

Before I could answer she butted in and said, "Oh it's
fine that his baby mama was staying in my house with those
kids."

"My kids!" I yelled correcting her.

She rolled her eyes and switched her weight to one leg,
"Only one is yours asshole."

Robert threw up his hands as I was prepping to charge
toward Gabrielle to whisper a few slanderous words in her
ear. Robert pushed me backwards turned and looked at
Gabrielle and told her to have a seat.

"What is going on with you and Gabrielle?" He asked walking to a quiet corner while examining the room. He began to frown and then slightly laughed out. "Why the hell is this lobby a damn blast from the past?"

"The hell if I know. I never thought I'd see the day Nitrah and Jazz were both in the same room with Dahlia."

Robert mumbled her name, "Dahlia. Haven't seen this woman in years. The other night when she showed up at the Rhapsody I didn't know what to think. Grateful we didn't have to talk, but now she is here in the same space again."

I watched my brother play the situation over in his head. He was struggling with his emotions a little. My brother was always the emotional type. He wasn't anything like how Tim and I were back in the day. He actually believed in monogamy. I mean; I did too at least now I did. That's why I married Gabrielle. To be faithful. But having this ring on my finger doesn't take the temptation away that I feel for Nitrah.

I patted Robert on the shoulder and said, "Man if we can just get through this week, we will be fine."

Robert stared at me blankly and said, "With you and Nitrah who are you fooling? That's why Gabrielle is tripping on you now. I told you the day you married that her, that the wrong woman was standing opposite of you."

I waved him off and said, "I don't want to hear that Robert." Just as we were about to get into another debate that we have performed a dozen times, I turned when I heard the announcement.

"The family to see Charmaine Wright. She is in the Rose Thornton room. It is the last room on the right." The

115

room grew quiet as Robert and I started to examine the room. Everyone else was shockingly doing the same thing: looking at each other. No one moved. No one took that first step. Not until Monica stood up from her seat.

. "I will lead the way," I said as I placed my hands in my pocket and signaled with my head for Gabrielle to come stand next to me.

Chapter 32

Jazzaray

Not trying to sound like the baby of the group, which I was, but I didn't want to go in there. I nudged Nitrah on the arm and whined. She took my hand in hers and asked for our guys, Cameron and Maxwell to walk behind us. I had already begun to sob. I bowed my head bringing my chin to my chest and took a deep breath. Maxwell placed his hands on my shoulders behind me and gave it a tight squeeze.

I eyed Tim and signaled with my head for him to come on. He was still seated in his chair as Dahlia and Monica made their way down the hallway.

"Tim, are you coming?"

He looked at me. His face was so blank that he nearly looked dead. My heart began to drop. I hadn't seen that look in Tim's eyes since the day I told him I wanted a divorce. I couldn't stand to see a grown man cry or in pain and in this moment he seemed so vulnerable. We all stopped as Nitrah bent down next to him.

"Tim I will hold her hand," Nitrah whispered.

He slowly turned his head to look at her. They were only inches away from each other's face as he said, "I could be the very reason why she is lying in that coffin."

I looked back and saw Denim walking towards us. He dropped his hand on Tim's shoulder and said, "I got you bro. We can walk together."

Personally, I had mixed emotions behind Tim's pain. I hurt for Charmaine. She was my friend and I used to love her but on the same end, I felt a certain way about Tim's pain over his dead lover. She was the same woman who betrayed me and our entire circle.

He reluctantly stood up and gave Denim a reassuring head nod. Finally, we all stood up to walk together but our nerves were suddenly jolted by a massive scream. My head turned quickly towards the cries and landed on Monica who had rushed through the doors.

We all quickened our steps and rushed toward the room that held Charmaine.

One step into the room and I felt my life slip under my knees. I grabbed Maxwell's arm for help. He embraced me as I cried out. At the very last minute, I realized that I was secretly hoping it wasn't going to be Charmaine lying dead in that coffin. When I realized it was her, my pain turned to anger. I pulled away from Maxwell, walked out of the room and I didn't look back.

Chapter 33

Dahlia

I tried for dear life to hold Monica upward, but I couldn't see past the tears and mucus that was taking over my face. She was becoming dead weight. I cried out for someone to help me and felt two men come and take her out of my arms. I didn't even bother to see who they were. They dragged her to the front pew and sat her down. She continued to weep and call Charmaine's name. I looked her and blew out hot air.

My chest was so tight and my throat felt like it was inches away from closing up. I turned my attention back to the white casket that held Charmaine. I guess actually seeing her lying there made it more real. She looked so much older than 32. Her hair was short and brittle, her skin was a little darker, and she was frail.

"What happened to her?" I heard Nitrah say as she walked up behind me.

I shook my head slowing and wiped my eyes with a napkin. "I don't know."

I felt Nitrah began to shake and start to whimper. I placed my hand on her shoulder and assured that she would be OK.

"Look at her Dahlia, just look at her. That isn't Charmaine. That's not the girl I remember." I looked at her and without even trying my eyes filled with tears. They were falling down my face as if they were rain drops.

I mouth the words to Nitrah, "I know. I know. I know." It was all that I could say. Nitrah and I eye's met. We stared at each other for the longest seconds of my life. My eyes said I want to be over all this beef. Her eyes said I refuse to hold on to a grudge after this. That's what our eyes said, but our mouths didn't move. Our stare was cut short when Tim walked over and placed his hand on Charmaine's brow.

I eyed him and the scene was so heartbreaking that I want to just scream out in frustration.

An attendee walk over to Nitrah and I and asked, "Are you the close to kin?"

Nitrah answered, "I guess so. She used to have a mother. Greta that was her name, but she has been gone. Gone for years. She had no sister, no brothers, no one else she spoke of."

I interjected and pointed to Monica, "Her oldest family is her, Monica." We all turned to look at Monica who had her head buried in her hands.

The attendee hesitated before saying, "Well, can you give this to her." She handed me a folder and walked away.

I opened it and began to suck my teeth in annoyance. "What is it?" Nitrah asked.

"It's an eight thousand dollar bill that's what it is. How the fuck is this bitch going to throw a bill at me when we have only been in here five minutes!" Nitrah began to try to shush me, but I was heated.

I felt someone rush up behind me and place their hands on my shoulder. "I got it Dahlia." Nitrah and I stared at Denim in shock and asked him if he was sure. He added, "I spend this much on a watch and that shit is unnecessary. This here is necessary. I'll do it for Charmaine." He took the folder and walked out of the room with it.

After he disappeared I turned back towards Nitrah who turned back towards me and without any hesitation she leaned in and hugged me. "It really is good to see you Dahlia." With a squeeze of my hand she smiled as did I and walked over to Cameron. I turned back towards Charmaine and just stared at her recounting our last conversation.

One year ago

"He doesn't seem that hot to me for you to be leaving Chicago for him. I mean damn, why so quickly anyway?"

"His name is Keith and he is a good guy. I met him when I was in D.C. on business. He got us a place already. He wants to start something fresh with me. Can't you just be happy for me?"

I watched Charmaine place her belongings in box after box. She had this angelic glow in her eyes and I knew she was genuinely happy, but I didn't understand why she was moving for a guy who she only met once two months ago.

"Look I know I can't sit here and tell you what to do because you're grown. But we left Fort Worth together to hold each other down. Now you're just going to leave me to Monica," I whined.

Monica walked in and laughed, "Girl let Charmaine be happy. Shit knowing her and how we got down since high school she'll be back. We always come back together." She plopped down on Charmaine's bed and took a scoop of the ice cream she was eating.

I waved her off, "Never mind how y'all roll. I'm here now and this shit is wack. What does this Keith guy do?"

"He is in advertising. But owns this art gallery with his sister, Nadine. I am going to work at the art gallery until he can get me a job at his advertising agency. We have a place in Alexandria. Look Dahlia I love you and I know you want the best for me. But after that mess with Tim and Jazz and damn near being back mailed by your sister, Joyclyn, I have been waiting for this moment."

I rolled my eyes and said, "What moment?"

"A moment to be happy. Can you just be happy for me?"

I paused and rolled my eyes again. I eyed Monica who winked at me to work my nerves. I threw a pillow at her. "Fine, but first things first. Once you get settled I am coming to visit. Deal?"

She walked over to me and towered over me giving me the biggest bear hug that her small frame could muster up. She gave me a wet kiss on my cheek and said, "I promise. I promise. I promise. Happy now?"

I wiped away her wet kiss and frowned. "For now I am. But I'll be seeing you in D.C. Ms. Iaminlove."

She left that weekend. Called a few times once she was there and then suddenly her phone disconnected. And then so was she, from my life. I hadn't seen her until this very moment. That was the moment I realized that her Prince Charming must have not been so sweet after all.

Chapter 34

Jazzaray

I lay still on my bed and allowed the smooth sounds of Avery Sunshine to coming through the system. I had stripped down to my panties and bra and turned my fan on full blast. I couldn't control the heat from my skin or the anxiety I was experiencing. My mind was racing a mile a minute. I couldn't stop thinking about the last time I had seen or spoken to Charmaine. It was a yelling match because I had discovered she was sleeping with my ex-husband even before he was my husband.

I heard footsteps closing in on me. I turn my head slightly to see who my intruder was. I smile lightly as his tall statue appeared in my door way. He had his dreads pulled back; he was dressed casually in this rare moment that he was home in the middle of the day.

"Hey babe," Maxwell said as he strolled in. His demeanor was softer than normal. I knew he was trying to act sweeter then sweet because of my vulnerability. I hadn't said much to him since we all left the funeral home. I left before anyone else did. I hated funeral homes, especially ones that held some of my history.

"How are you are feeling Jazz baby?" He leaned over and pecked my lips. I lay in the middle of our gigantic king size bed sinking deep into our plush comforter and just smiled.

"I'll live." The words began to pierce at my heart as soon as they left my lips. I was living and Charmaine wasn't.

Maxwell placed his hands on my shoulders and gave them a tight squeeze. "You are tense. Should I rub my baby down?" He bent down and whispered merely inches away from my lips. I nodded my head yes and turned over on my stomach allowing my bare ass to be the center of his view.

Maxwell was my Heaven on Earth. I loved him more than I could have ever imagined loving anyone. He had saved me years ago when I was being attacked by my ex-boyfriend who I accidently killed. He had saved me when I was ending a tumultuous marriage, he had saved me when I was experiencing panic attacks, and he was here being my savior again when the guilt and sadness was weighing heavy on my heart.

"I feel guilty." I whispered to him. Large tears swelled in my eyes and fell down my cheek.

He towered himself over me climbing into our bed and brought my head down to lay it on his chest. "Babe I know I can't magically change the way you feel, but I am not going to allow you think to that the way you feel is wrong. The last time you saw Charmaine was when you discovered she was with Tim. I understand your torn emotions. Jazz you're human so don't beat yourself over for that."

There was a long pause and the room was silent except for the fan blowing. I rose my head up and said, "I need a run. I'm going to go run at the lake. Can you stay here with the kids?" Maxwell eyed me and gave me the 'are you serious' look. "Go on I got the kids."

I hopped out of the bed, placed on my running gear, and headed outside. The summer's evening air was surprisingly cool as I made my way onto the sidewalk. I placed my iPod on full blast and gripped my stun gun in my right hand. I never left home without it. With each step I stomped away my anger towards Charmaine and I think for a moment I allowed my heart to just cry out for her.

Chapter 35

Nitrah

"Don't eat up all of my fries Denim. Besides don't you think this fried food is bad on this physique you're trying to maintain?" I blushed dropping a fry from William's Chicken in my mouth.

"So you're watching huh?" He asked with a cocky smirk spread thin across his face.

"Nope. It's just hard to miss it when you insist on rolling up your sleeves and flexing your skinny ass arms."

He laughed throwing a napkin in my face. "Skinny. Ha!" He took a huge bite of his chicken then asked, "So you and Troy huh? Man you two had me on a merry-go-round years ago. I must admit you were hard to get over."

Pointing at myself I quizzed, "I was hard? No you were hard. You and your cheating ways. You are such a whore." I laughed taking a huge swallow of my lemonade. "And what do you mean me and Troy?"

"I know you and I know that you were a little disheveled when you came and met us out on the patio at the Lyrical Lounge. You and Troy had disappeared to the back. The same way I use to get you sometimes."

I stared at him blankly waiting for him to say anything else but he didn't. "He's married now and I can't get right."

"Well, Ms. Can't Get Right what are you going to go in this situation? Ten years of this back and forth and you would expect for me to be the last one to say anything, but you need to make up your mind. Plus I thought you were all in love with that Cameron nigga. Who by the way, ain't got shit on me!"

I rolled my eyes and said, "I don't know why you are comparing a faithful, hardworking man to your million dollar bank account whoremongering self."

"Damn Nitrah, you always got to put me down. But I still love you though." He winked.

I waved him off and continued to eat my food and asked, "If you noticed do you think anyone else noticed? The last thing I want to do is be in his wife's face smiling and shit."

"Now you see why Gabrielle always acts a fool when you and the kids come around. She isn't stupid, she knows."

"Well Denim if she knows of this chemistry that Troy and I have why does she stay?"

"The same reason why women stay with me. They think they can change me. It's a sad truth, but all you women think you can change a man and you can't. I mean I can and I did for a little bit with you but then I fell back into my routine. I wasn't ready and still ain't. Probably never will be."

I leaned back in my chair and said, "I was in town just to see family and I ended up seeing my former best friend in a coffin and sleeping with my baby daddy. This is a hot ass mess."

Denim grew quiet as he continued to munch on his food. "Fool did you hear me," I yelled out.

"Yeah, yeah, yeah I heard you. I got a show tonight at Club Dre. I know you and the ladies may not feel up to it but invite them out. You all have a depressing week ahead with this funeral and all, so why not? Come out, sit in VIP, drink on me, dance, and do whatever it is y'all do to have fun."

I raised an eye brow. "Can I bring a date?"

Denim stopped midway in his feast on his next piece of chicken, "Cameron or Troy?"

I looked up to the sky and pondered his question, "You'll see when I walk through the door."

Chapter 36

Troy

Gabrielle walked down our terrace slowly one step at a time without as much as a word. Her demeanor was calm, but I knew better than that. This was the quiet before the storm. The moment before yet another argument. I was over it. I was over this. And I think she knew that it was about that time.

"Are you ok down here? You haven't come upstairs yet?"

I took another swallow of the brown liquor I had poured myself and grunted. "I'm fine."

She walked behind me placing her hands on my shoulders and began to give an impromptu massage.

"You ever wonder what life would be like if you would have made different choices, considering its outcome and circumstances?" I asked.

She stopped midstride on my shoulders and asked, "Like what?"

"Just in general Gabbie, have you?"

"Of course I have regrets, but I stopped making them years ago the day I decided to grow up." She took her hands off of my shoulders and stood up. I could hear her walking around the couch finally taking a seat on our love seat across from me. "What are you thinking about Troy?"

Imagine the reaction my wife would have if I told her the deepest desires of my heart. I took a vow to honor her and to be true. But the more and more I thought about my honor and truth, it always lied with Nitrah, especially when it came to our daughter. I always put Nina first even before Gabrielle. Let's face it that was my child and I held a sense of devotion to Nitrah because of that. Somewhere deep within I felt Gabrielle knew this.

"I am just thinking. Today was a rough one. I think everyone expected to go to that funeral home and not actually see Charmaine in that casket. But when reality settled in, so did everyone's pain," I whispered. I had my eyes focused on my now empty glass of liquor.

"You seem pretty crushed over a woman you weren't that close to." Gabrielle slouched back in her seat and folded her arms across her chest.

I gave her the side-eye and studied her emotions quickly. She held an attitude and once again I knew I was going to be in for an argument if I continue to talk on the matter at hand. But being who I was, and currently not giving a damn I continued. "It's more than just Charmaine, Gabrielle."

"Is it your precious Nitrah?" She mocked.

"Why do you always take it there? Gabbie, I don't feel like having one of your random beef announcements about my baby's mother."

"Why do you always get sensitive when I mention her huh?" She jumped to her feet nearly charging at me. I jumped upward as well to brace myself for her to curse me out in her native tongue or to invade my personal space.

"Nitrah is family."

Gabrielle poked her chest out and sucked her teeth, "And I'm not? I am your wife."

Waving my hands I said aggravated, "Gabrielle I just witnessed one of my former friends lying in her coffin. Almost every friend of mine is affected by this in a bad way. I have to be stronger inside and out for everyone and I come home to this bull shit. Like are you serious right now? I don't give a fuck about what you want to scream about now. I don't." I screamed at the top of my lungs and threw my hands at her. In no way was I going to hit her but she reacted as if she thought I would. I shook my head at her in disappointment and annoyance and climbed up the stairs two at time. I marched into my bathroom to cut the shower on steam. After all I needed this shower to relax my mind, muscles, and mostly to wash away any evidence of Nitrah. Today was one interesting day.

Chapter 37

Nitrah

I lay across my old bed staring at the ceiling as I used to do back in high school. My room wasn't too much different from how it looked back then. Mama didn't do too much redecorating. I looked up to see Cameron walking through the door.

"Hey babe, Mama is about done with those chicken and dumplings. She is in there with Jazz's mom mapping out the funeral."

I shook my head OK. "Good I can't wait to eat. Where are the kids?"

"Across the street playing with some other kids. You OK now?" I didn't answer Cameron as he bent down and pecked my lips finally laying down next to me on what was one of the world's oldest full size mattresses.

"I just want to eat," I whispered. My voice was that of a whining teenager.

Cameron rose up from the bed and walked over to my old dresser. My prom picture sat there in the middle. I wore the loudest pink dress you could think of. I laughed out and said, "Hey that was the late 90s don't judge me."

Cameron laughed and then proceeded to open the top drawer. "What's all of this stuff?"

I look focused my eyes on what he was looking at and found a box of old letters. Most were folded up in little squares and triangles. I gasped in embarrassment, "Oh my gosh! I didn't know I still had these inhere." Sitting up on the bed I took the box in my hand as Cameron took a seat next to me.

"What is it?"

"A box of old letters from like middle school and high school, maybe college too." I started to fumble and go through the various papers. I giggled and gasped at many of them once I remembered the substance of the letters. Most were gossip.

"Any love letters?"

I push a few papers back and said, "My college letters have to be back here. I remember organizing those years ago. My hands landed on a green piece of paper with silver lettering. It was a letter I remembered writing in college. I pulled it out and gripped it in between my fingers.

"What's that one?" Cameron asked reading my reaction to it.

My mouth fell open for what seemed like an eternity as the day I received this letter replayed in my head. "It was from Charmaine. My sophomore year."

October 1999

So don't worry about yesterday. I promised that I was going to get Greta to let me use her car but because she was too drunk to remember that she said yes, I will just have to take it once she passes out. I heard from Angelica, the newspaper editor, that you can place your poem in the paper that way when he gets it and reads the games high lights you can point it out to him you know. Don't worry about it. I will work something out. Once he reads your poem, he will fall putty into your hands and ask you to the homecoming dance. I'll see to it. Anyway, heading to my chemistry class and I pray I don't cuss out Professor Wilkes today. He works my damn nerve. Write back and tell me when you want to put the poem in the paper.

Char

I didn't notice that I had tears streaming down my face until Cameron took his hand and wiped them across my cheeks. "This was about you, how ironic." I laughed in between my tears. Cameron took the letter into his hands and read through it quickly.

"I remember this. The poem, but you didn't tell me you wanted me to take you to the dance."

I took the letter back and stuff it back into the box. "That's ancient history now. Instead you took the whore of the class. Bet you got lucky that night."

Cameron blew out air and laughed. He raised an eyebrow and asked, "She mentioned a Greta, who was that?"

I paused and reflected on Greta. I never knew her well. When we did go around her she always walked back to her room and shut her door. "It was her mother. She left her years ago."

"Left Charmaine? Like where is she now?"

"The hell if I know. Charmaine hadn't even spoken of her name since college and since forever it's been like Greta never existed. I totally didn't think of her until this letter now. I wonder where she is? I should ask Monica."

I heard Mama's voice scream out, "Go get the kids and tell them the food is ready!" Cameron and I rose up simultaneously and headed towards the front of the house, but not before I placed the box of letters back where it belonged hidden away.

Chapter 38

Dahlia

Robert had managed to slip a piece of paper into my hand before we left the funeral home. It contained seven digits. I sent a text it and he replied with an address and so here I sat. It was a small café in Arlington not too far from the Rangers ballpark. I ordered a strawberry banana smoothie while I waited for him to show up.

In a matter of minutes I felt a hand land on my shoulder. I jerked back in shock. "Robert you scared me." I said trying to regain my composure.

"Sorry about that." He bent down to kiss me on the cheek and asked, "Are you ok?"

I blankly stared at him and said, "Three days until the funeral and then I will be. How are you and the Mrs.?"

He smiled a little bit almost letting out a laugh and turned his attention to the menu. "Think I am going to get me a basket of wings. One sec." He walked up to the counter and ordered his wings and was back in front of me in a matter of minutes. "You look good."

"Thanks." It fell silent for what seemed like an annoying hour of just waiting for him to get to the point.

"And…" I said not hiding the fact that the mystery of the visit was working my nerves.

"I figured I would meet up with you since the first time we've seen each other in years. I have a wife on my shoulder. I mean no one has heard from you in a long time."

"Yeah I wanted to keep it that way. You moved on from this place."

"But this place is home." He shot back.

"It was at one point when life made sense. Now it's just a memory of what use to be. All of that I used to know is dead and gone."

"So what's new with you anyhow? I know since we saw you at the Rhapsody, no one could tell each other the mystery of your comeback."

I laughed out and said, "Were you sent by everyone else to pick my brain for some gossip?"

"Nope, to be honest I just wanted to see you. My eyes haven't set sight on you in years and if only I got a few minutes of your time I wanted to just talk. To see how you are doing."

"Well, I see you are doing fine. You and your brother decided to settle down huh?"

"I started dating my wife not too long after you left. Troy got back with an old friend and married her. Life went on and changed you know. Jazz and Max have the new baby, Nitrah has the new baby, and then there's you now."

I rolled my eyes quickly replying, "I have a nice job in Chicago."

"Chicago? That's where you have been?"

"Yep!" I arrogantly starred him in the eyes without as much as a blink. I didn't shy away, I didn't flinch and to my surprise neither did he. It was like he was challenging my boldness. I got the idea that he wasn't buying my hard ass persona. After the longest uncomfortable minutes of staring at him in his eyes I had to look away. "What?" I frowned asking him feeling defeated.

"You seem angry." The worker called out his name and without giving me a chance to reply to his declaration of my feelings he jumped up to retrieve his wings. Before he was back and his ass hit the seat I blurted out my attempt to correct his announcement.

"I am not angry. I am annoyed."

Pouring hot sauce over his wings he replied nonchalantly, "Annoyed at what."

Hitting my hand on the table I yell, "Dammit Robert stop fucking with them damn wings and my emotions over here! Why did you ask me to meet you?"

His head shot up from his basket of wings and landed on me, "A little antsy aren't we? Why do I have to have a motive to want to meet up? I mean it's been years and suddenly you're here. Sue me."

I pushed back my seat and stood up, "I don't have time for a social visit. Once Charmaine is buried I am out of here."

"Just like that?"

"Just like that!"

Chapter 39

Jazzaray

I walked into the steak house and asked one of the hosts where my party was sitting. I followed behind her admiring the fish tanks that were embedded in the walls and portraits of prominent locals who had eaten here. Finally we walked up a stairwell to where I noticed Nitrah and Dahlia sitting.

I smiled slightly and made my way over to them. "Hey ladies." I bent down hugging each of them briefly and sat down scooting my chair as close as I could to the table.

"You look nice," Dahlia said taking a sip of her white wine.

I eyed her drink and said, "I definitely need one of those."

"We've only been here for about ten minutes or so and we haven't ordered yet. Just our drinks. I'm not going to lie Dahlia and I had an awkward moment of silence for about five minutes," Nitrah lightly laughed.

Dahlia joined in and laughed, "Oh you noticed huh?"

"Well in that case let me add more to this awkward moment. I turned in my seat to directly face Dahlia and say, "It's been a long time."

Dahlia reached up and placed her hand on top of mine. "Yes it has. You ladies look great though. Not a day over twenty-five."

I laughed out and say, "Well gee thanks. I am going to enjoy my last year in my twenties and toast it up as soon as the waiter comes back to take my drink order."

Nitrah pushed herself back into her seat and said, "I'm not going to lie. It's kind of weird to be here with you two like this." Her eyes trailed to an empty chair that was seated across from me. The fourth chair.

I turned my head as I instantly picked up on what Nitrah meant and then the significance of that empty chair. "She was supposed to be here," Dahlia whispered.

"I keep thinking about the last thing I said to her all those years ago. I know what she did to me was wrong. I know I should feel hate for the woman who was sleeping with my husband the whole time we were together. But I don't. I am human and this woman was a part of my life. I wouldn't wish this on anyone."

Nitrah eyed Dahlia, "Jazz and I hadn't spoken to her in years, but what about you? Until now we hadn't heard from you either."

Dahlia took a sip of her wine and said, "It was about a year ago. We both were living in Chicago. We had stayed close long after leaving here."

Nitrah cut her off and said, "Oh really?"

I interjected and said, "Let her finish Nitrah."

Dahlia continued, "You two were here with your unforgiving hearts and we were in Chicago escaping our pasts. That's the truth. That was life, you know?"

"We were unforgiving to the blatant lies and the deceit. Like you both were fucking our men! Like who does that?" Nitrah blurted.

Dahlia turned her head and blew out hot air. "It's a lot you two don't know. I have been replaying shit in my head too trying to make sense of all of this, but keep coming up short."

I asked, "So a year ago what happened? Why was it a year ago when you last saw her?"

"She left to be with a man she fell in love with. His name was Keith. That's all I knew. He lived out in D.C. She called me when she first left, but by several months ago nothing. I hadn't heard a peep until now. Until I found out she was dead."

"Something had to have happened in between that time. I don't get it." Nitrah added. We fell silent again.

"I got the bill on the funeral and was wondering," Dahlia added.

Nitrah interrupted her and said, "Denim took care of it. Let's order something to eat y'all all of this talk is wreaking havoc on my stomach."

"I agree because we have to meet everyone over Nitrah's Mama's house in a bit. She planned a cookout for everyone."

"Everyone?" Dahlia quizzed.

"Hell no you can't bring Monica's trifling ass," I shot back.

Nitrah added, "To my Mama's house? Monica can go get on her knees somewhere and do what she does best. Suck a d..."

"OK," Dahlia said cutting us off. "Fine I won't tell her."

I mumbled, "What a friend to keep in your corner by the way."

It was a matter of seconds that felt like minutes when Dahlia added, "She is more like me than you think."

I didn't say it out loud, but I totally agreed with what she just said and it wasn't in a good way.

Chapter 40

Nitrah

After I pulled my hair back into a bun, I wrapped some loose hairs around my fingers to give them a little curl. I was slipping into my sandals whens Nina burst into my room. "Umm, can you knock? What's up?"

"Pops is here and he brought Ms. Latina," Nina blurted out.

I eyed and shushed her, "Don't repeat what I call her. Stay in your place Nina. That's your Daddy's wife."

She plops down on the bed and says, "Yeah for now. That lady doesn't like me. And when she is speaking that foreign language Mama she is talking about me. Wait till I am as tall as her I'm going to speak something back."

I jerked my head back towards her and said, "You are a little too grown for me. As long as she respects you in English and keeps her hands to herself you do the same. You got me?"

She nodded her head and strolled out of the room as Cameron made his way in, "Nina just walked past me switching like she is 18. I'm on the edge of jumping on her back."

I laughed, "You wouldn't believe how she was just in here talking. That girl isn't even a teen yet and already giving me the blues."

Cameron took a seat at the edge of the bed and cupped his hands together and starred up at me. "Troy is here."

I went back over to the mirror to take a last glance at my outfit and said, "Yeah, Nina just told me." The silence in the room created an uncomfortable vibe that was so thick that I swear it was sucking up all of the oxygen out of the room. I turned my body around to face him, "Yes?"

"I don't like when he is around. You know what."

"Cam, you have to seriously get over it. He is family. Been family for years now and because we share Nina he will be here and so will you."

"He needs to tell my son to stop calling him Pops."

"Little Cameron has known Troy since he was in diapers, he is his sister's Dad. He just calls him that because Nina does. He is family to him too you know." I placed my hands on my hip and gave Cameron the 'are you serious' look.

"Nina doesn't call me Dad."

I rolled my eyes and threw my hands up in the air. "By the time you came along she was set on calling one man Daddy. Like can we really get over this? This a never ending battle with you. I swear men can be sensitive." I whispered the end of my statement to, of course, avoid an argument. But Cameron's big eared ass heard me and it spun into a whole new discussion.

I raised my hand up to stop the madness before it began. "The funeral is tomorrow. I just want to chill with my friends and family and not be interrogated on some high school mess."

Cameron stood up slowly his tall six foot frame nearly doubling my height and looked down at me. "Oh yeah I forgot to mention to you that you left this on the bathroom floor the other day."

He reached from behind his back and I looked down and noticed the dress I had on the day…..my mind raced back to the day I allowed Troy inside of me. I immediately put on my A game face and said, "Oh yeah. Thanks." I went to reach for it but he pulled back.

"You may want to get that stain removed." I raised an eyebrow and just as I was about to ask him what did he mean he threw the dress in my face and My nieces R'Mani and Vivian singing Jesus is the Light! I love them so much! http://www.youtube.com/watch?v=HAyaQUxYG7swalked off. Yanking it off I jerked around to yell at him, but all I saw was a shadow of where he once stood.

I gripped the dress in my hand and looked down at it. I pulled it open and held it up in the air in search for what the hell he meant. Then my eyes landed on the bottom of the dress. There it was a stain and there was no denying what it was.

Troy had ejaculated on my clothes. That's a residue I knew I couldn't hide or lie about and now Cameron knew and I could only imagine who he thought it was from. "Damn!" I said to myself.

"What's wrong girl?" Jazz's head poked in from around the corner. "Come on out. Everyone is here."

I buried the dress at the bottom of my suitcase and followed Jazz out. I knew today was only going to give me a headache.

Chapter 41

Troy

"Your boy just walked out." After having fixed myself two plates of Nitrah's mom's food, I walked over to her to see what was up. I hadn't spoken to her and I knew her time in Fort Worth was winding down.

"He's a big boy." Nitrah shot back.

"So what did you cook on the menu by the way?" She rolled her eyes at me knowing that I knew she didn't care to cook and that her cooking today would be a straight up miracle.

I glanced over and noticed Nitrah's brother, Jailen, get up and turn on the radio. I turned my head back and smirked.

Nitrah shook her head and laughed, "Don't go there we are not about to do that.

"Come on babe. I missed you," I whined.

Nitrah leaned in closer with her eyes as big as they could get and asked, "Are you crazy to be flirting with me with your wife here? Get your ass away Troy before she starts to speak in that language no one understands."

I pulled at her hand and then noticed her mother walking towards her, "Hey Mama, let's get down." I grabbed her hand too and with a Ms. Hill on both arms I went to the center of the living room and we danced to Luther Vandross "Bad Boy". Mama laughed out as she began to swing out.

I placed my hands on Nitrah's hips and guided her to match my rhythm. I yelled out over the music for everyone to get up. Jazz and Maxwell joined in and one by one the others followed. And it seemed like we all had the desire for this moment to last for eternity, but it was only a few minutes before we heard a knock on the door.

Jailen ran over to turn down the music as Mama made her way over to the door. I let loose of Nitrah and went to search for Gabrielle. I found her on the patio seated, her arms folded across her chest as she stared at the numerous kids playing in the backyard.

"Hey babe."

She turned her head, eyed me and then turned her focus back on the kids playing, "You seem to be enjoying yourself."

I took a seat next to her, "You would too if you came inside."

"I don't even know why we are here."

"Because this is my family," I said.

She turned her body in her chair and jerked her head around, "You're a lie! It's your daughter's family. Not yours."

I rose up to walk away before yet another one of rants began. "I don't feel like dealing with this shit. Like enough is enough."

Gabrielle laughed and added, "Yeah I agree, enough is enough. Just like the stain that Cameron mentioned was on Nitrah's dress. I wonder where that came from?"

Chapter 42

Jazzaray

As I walked out of Nitrah's mom's house my cell rang. I flipped it open and answered, "Hello. Yea Hello?" I pushed the receiver further into my ear to get a better listen. When that didn't work I walked further away from the front door.

"Jazz, I need you to come pick me up."

"Tim, boy where are you? You were supposed to be here hours ago. The food is practically gone."

"I need you to come get me Jazz." Tim repeated himself.

His tone was too mellow and nonchalant for my liking. That's how I knew something was wrong. I quizzed him and asked, "What happened now?" I had never told Maxwell, but a few times in the past year I had to get Tim out of jail. Once for fighting in the club and the rest for DUI's. I was hoping it was neither this time. "What did you do?"

"I'm at the corner of Miller and Berry. Can you be here in thirty?"

I blew out hot air and agreed to be there on time. I walked back in and searched for Maxwell, "I am going to go make a store run for Mama. I will be right back."

Rushing out of the door after he said OK, I bumped into Dahlia who was making her way in. "Oh hey. I didn't think you were coming."

"Well I wasn't at first, but decided why not. My time here is almost done."

"Where's your girl Monica?"

"She is at the funeral home, dropping off Char's dress."

"Oh!" An awkwardly silent ten seconds passed when Dahlia continued, "Headed out?"

"Tim is in some type of trouble, so I am off to be Captain Save a Hoe again." I threw my hands up in the air to demonstrate my annoyance.

"I can ride with you if you want. I mean I don't mind." I looked her over and played with the idea for a few seconds before I reluctantly agreed to let her ride with me. We sped off from Nitrah's mom's house headed straight for the highway.

In less than twenty I was pulling up into a Shell gas station and noticed Tim leaned up against his truck talking to a guy whose back was to me. I parked and hopped out alongside with Dahlia. I threw my hand up in the air and yelled, "Tim what's going on?"

With the screech in my voice at an all-time high, the guy he was talking to turned around. That's when Dahlia and I both zoomed in on him and my mouth dropped. "Well I'll be damn."

I looked over to Dahlia and laughed and she looked back at me in shock and said, "Is that Michael?"

I rushed up to him in excitement and threw my arms around his neck. I hadn't seen him in person in so many years, but he looked the same. He was still tall and gorgeous with that smooth beige skin. He was Troy's friend from back in the day. Maybe ten years ago. He also had a thing for Nitrah, which is why they stopped being friends.

Dahlia followed up behind me and hugged Michael as Tim began to interrogate me, "Are you rolling with her now? Is her trifling friend with you?"

I rolled my eyes and shushed him, "Michael what are you doing here?"

"I am in town with my family for Charmaine's funeral."

"Family?" Dahlia asked.

"Yep got married a little while ago and even got a second baby on the way. You'll meet her tomorrow at the funeral."

I asked him, "Who told you about Charmaine?"

"I stay in contact with friends and family here and there and heard it through the grapevine. I knew all you ladies would be back and thought it would be right to come pay my respects. "

"Have you seen Nitrah?" Dahlia asked.

"I did a couple years back at her lounge. We talked, exchanged contact info and that was that. She had told me about her new son and how she and Troy were co-parenting." He rubbed his hand across his beard and reminisced. "Man it seems like yesterday I used to run these streets with you Tim."

I laughed and said, "Tim is still running these streets with a line of hoes behind him." I took my attention back to Tim and curiously asked, "Why did you call me out here again?"

"Tim dropped his head turning his attention back to his shoes. I walked up to him and pushed him in his chest, "I know you heard me, what's going on Tim?"

Michael cut in and said, "He had a flat. I was near and helped him out."

I raised an eyebrow and turned my attention back to Michael, "I know you're lying and I know this Negro done went and did something stupid that he will be begging for me to get him out of later. But if you say so." I hugged him goodbye, gave him my number, and told him I would see him and his family tomorrow.

"Michael is going to be in the same building as Troy. This is going to be good." Dahlia said as we hopped back into my car.

"Sure is and Tim is lying, but right now I don't care enough to find out why. Let's run by the store and get some soda's and head back to Ms. Hill's house.

Chapter 43

Tim

I watched Jazz pull out of the parking lot before I turned my attention back to Mike. I hadn't seen him in a few and lo and behold he spots me from across the street at Robinson's Bar B Cue. I extended my fist for him to pound.

Accepting my gesture he said, "Follow me across the street so we can sit and talk, cool?"

"Yeah man that's cool." I hopped back into my truck put it in reverse and made my way across the street to the mom and pop soul food restaurant.

I met Mike inside and ordered me a plate since I know I was going to miss out on Nitrah's mom's cooking. "You are looking like money Mike." I said, once we were both seated.

"And you... well you look about the same, that's a good thing. What are you doing these days?"

"Still in construction. Actually working on a new restaurant right now for Jazz's dude."

"Her husband?"

"Yeah!"

"So you work for her husband? That's... well how is that working out?"

I shrugged my shoulder, "It gives me check." The server came over and placed my plate in front of me and I began to dig in. "So how long are you in town for?"

"Just a couple days. My wife is from here too so we wanted to see family."

"Where do you live at now?"

"In Sacramento."

"Oh word? Yeah you always loved the West Coast. You like it out there?"

"Yeah the Bay area is a different world from Texas you know."

"So you got any more kids besides Tim Jr." Michael laughed. I laughed a little too. We both knew I changed women like they bought our new Jordan's.

"Nah, just Tim Jr. I'm good with one baby mama."

"I'm kind of sad to see that you and Jazz never got back together though. You were in love with that girl. That I do remember."

"I was, but a nigga like me will never get it right. I know and understand my selfish ways. Maybe one day I'll change. Just not today." I dig into my food some more as our conversation grew to an awkward silence.

"So why did y'all break up?" Michael quizzed. In that moment I remembered just how long he's been out of the circle. He didn't know. And I didn't want to remember, but as soon as he asked I remembered the last time I saw Charmaine.

ð ð ð

"You seem tense today. What's going on?" Charmaine walked around the bed and took a seat next to me. She had been back in town from Chicago for two weeks now and we hadn't left each other's sight more than ten minutes. I lay across the bed on my stomach as she straddled my back. I could hear her pouring lotion into her hands to massage my shoulders as I had requested.

"Work site is slow. No money coming in and Jazz keeps hinting that she expects this type of shit from me. I may not have been a good husband, but I am always there for my son."

"I agree with you on that one. I mean I just don't get it."

"You don't get what?"

"You wanted Jazz so badly that I even helped you get her. I recruited all my friends to do your dirty work and only for you to fuck that up. What was all of that for?"

I turned over on my back so quickly that Charmaine fell to the right of me nearly hitting the floor. "Are you questioning me?"

Charmaine looked away and mumbled under her breath. When I asked her to repeat herself and speak up she jerked her head back towards me and said, "I am just calling it how I see it. You did all of that and for what?"

"Don't worry about why the fuck I did anything. You just do what the hell I say and make sure you do it right."

Charmaine rose up from the bed and walked over to the bedroom mirror. I studied her demeanor as she looked at herself in the mirror and asked, "Is one of your crying spells coming? I swear you can be an emotional wreck sometimes."

She jerked around and screamed, "How can you not care about me? The only person who would do anything for you!"

I waved my hand at her and fell back down on the bed and started to search for the remote. "Don't start Charmaine."

"Don't start! You have some nerve to tell me that. I haven't talked to my friends in years. I have no one and you tell me to don't start. I should just kill you."

I jumped up and screamed, "Bitch threaten me again and see what happens! Ain't no one ever forced your ass to do anything! And look, you're still here. I met your ass when you were dark and ugly. Helped you build your self-esteem and now you want to act like you all high and mighty. Shut up with that shit and be grateful."

Charmaine picked up a glass and before she had the chance to throw it and hit me I jumped up and rolled off onto the floor. My eyes landed on the spot the where the glass hit the wall and shattered. My reaction was quick. I jumped up and marched over towards her. She began to push backwards into the dresser and extended her hands in hopes that I didn't come near her.

I grabbed her shoulders and shook her hard while yelling whatever I thought of at the top of my lungs. Charmaine squeezed her eyes tightly and tears began to seep through her lids. I picked her up and threw her down on the bed. I showed no remorse as I watched her head dangle like a doll. The room fell to a dead silence. I couldn't hear anything, but the rapid breaths going in and out of my lungs. I watched her and waited for her next move.

She pushed herself up on her right elbow and began to mutter, "You are the only consistent thing in my life and I don't know why. You don't give a fuck about me."

I didn't say anything as she proclaimed my feelings for her. However, I am going to keep it real. I loved Charmaine, but not like she loved me. I cared about her wellbeing like if she was breathing or not. But anything further was just to get what I wanted out of her. She did whatever I wanted when I wanted. I wasn't happy that everyone in her life had alienated because of the choices I asked her to make. But like I said I didn't force her to do anything. She just did it.

She began to rub her stomach and then clinch it. "I gave up a child because you were so stuck on Jazz. You swore up and down that a baby by me would ruin everything and I listened. I allowed you to convince me to abort my child and now I have no one. I am all the way in Chicago with no one."

I said, "You have Monica. And didn't I tell you not to mention the abortion? It never happened and never will again."

Charmaine cried out, "I hate you! I hate you!" It seemed like she repeated those words to me over and over a hundred times as I began to put my clothes back on one garment at a time. Once I was fully dressed I walked towards the hotel room door and opened it. Before stepping out of the room I turned around and, "Good luck Charmaine. With everything." And I walked away. That was the last time that I saw her alive.

ðÐð

I had finished my food as Michael waited for me to tell him why Jazz and I didn't work out. I was thinking maybe I needed a change of scenery too. Life here was getting old and tired. I was ready for something new.

I looked at Michael and said seriously, "I cheated. You know how I do. I changed for a minute but then went right back to being me." Michael didn't do anything but nod his head. We finished up our talk in half an hour before we went our separate ways.

As I drove my truck back to my apartment, I called one of my ladies to meet me there. Not only did I need some company; but a good fuck would help derail my mind from thinking about Charmaine and how it all ended. I didn't want to get out again today knowing that tomorrow we would bury Charmaine.

Chapter 44

Dahlia

I stood in the doorway of the funeral home for some fresh air. We had about thirty minutes before anyone of us could walk into the room where we could say our last goodbyes. Monica walked up to me and squeezed my hand. "It's almost over," I whispered.

I told her I would be back as I walked out and found a clean spot on the curb to take a seat. I needed some time away from the madness to clear my head. Just when I found my peace I heard a voice say, "Why are you sitting out here?"

My eyes trailed all the way up the body and my eyes landed on Robert. I rolled my eyes and asked, "Where's your wife?"

He voluntarily sat down next to me and placed his hand on my knee, "She's inside prepping to take a seat. How are you doing?"

"I am just fine Robert."

"You can talk to me you know."

"Look, what is up? Why are you in my face right now?"

Robert removed his hand from my knee and clenched his hands together, "I'm not your enemy Dahlia. I am a man who is human. I once loved you and I care about if you're ok."

"I am not the one lying in a coffin. Charmaine is. Charmaine is dead and no one even knew where she was for a damn year. I can't take this." I dropped my head into my lap and cried out. I felt Robert place his hands on the back of my neck and give it a tight squeeze.

"I know, I know and I hate that we have to go through this Dahlia. But life sometimes throws us a curve ball we can't knock out of the park. We got to try to hit it anyway and get through it. You will get through this too."

I didn't fight the fact that I felt a sense of protection with Robert sitting next to me. I hadn't been held, hugged, or consoled in any way since finding out about Charmaine. My mind was still trying to grasp the fact that she was gone.

I lifted my head upward and asked Robert, "Do you mind if I lay my head on your shoulder?"

He smiled at me and nodded his head. His yellow complexion was now a shade darker. He wore a full beard and had a head full of hair that was an inch off his scalp and curly. He smelled better then heaven and his broad shoulders were perfect for me. Better than any pillow ever invented. True, he is my ex Troy's brother. They're both my ex. But if I had to choose all over again I would choose Robert.

Chapter 45

Troy

I asked Gabrielle to go inside and be seated because I was assigned to be one of the pallbearers. I saw Robert and Dahlia sitting on the curb so I walked over and took a seat next to my brother. I patted his shoulder for reassurance and then leaned over and placed my hand on Dahlia's knee. "Are you going to be ok?"

She nodded her head up and down, but she didn't remove it from Robert's shoulder. I turned my attention back to my brother and we gave each other a reassuring head nod. We knew today was going to be emotional for our ladies. Thinking of the ladies made me go out on a search for Nitrah. I dropped my hands into the pockets of my suit and walked around to the parking lot. I spotted her leaned up against her car on her cell.

I marched over to her and immediately became concerned when I saw she was arguing. The protector in me took off into first gear. I stood in front of her and mouthed the words "Are you ok?"

She waved me off and nodded her head yes, but her eyes said another thing. I walked around her car and saw

Cameron Jr. and Nina seated in the back. "Hey, why haven't y'all gotten out yet?"

Cameron replied, "Mama said to wait in the car so we can walk in together."

I looked over to Nina and said, "You look pretty baby girl."

She turned her head and eyed me, "So Pops you and Mama got Mr. Cameron upset. I heard him talking about you this morning."

"What? Nina, mind out of grown folks business. Go ahead and get out of the car and walk your brother inside. Find your Aunt Jazz." I pulled open the door after stumbling over my words. Nina caught me off guard with her accusatory tone.

After Nina and Cameron Jr. were safely out of earshot, I turned my attention back to Nitrah who had hung up the phone. "So what's going on?"

She walked around me opened her car door to get her purse. I repeat my question after locking the door behind her. She jerked around and calmly said, "I can't believe I am back at square one because of your ass again. This shit is getting too old."

She turned around on her heels to leave, but I reached and grabbed her elbow to turn her back around, "Are you mad at me? What's going on?"

She laughed awkwardly and said, "Dude let go of my arm. You fucked me and Cameron figured that shit out. Every time I am near you shit goes wrong in my world."

I released her arm and rubbed my hand across my chin, "Oh so that is what Gabrielle was hinting at. He must have told her. And how did he figure it out? I mean no one saw us."

"I had a stain on my dress that you so tackily left behind."

I held up my hands in surrender. "Like woe Nitrah, why are you mad at me? I didn't force anything. We both knew what was up. We both wanted it."

She tried to turn around, but I jumped in her path and forced her to look at me, "Am I wrong?"

Nitrah rolled her eyes and looked at me with annoyance. I gave her a sly smirk to tap on her last nerve as she replied, "We always want each other and something is wrong with that picture."

I took two steps closer to her. So close that her breast brushed across my suit jacket. The tip of her nose was mere inches away from my chin as I lowered my head and nearly matched my lips with hers and said, "What are we going to do about that?"

In a blink of an eye I heard behind me, "Yo Troy, what's up?" I stepped backwards, but was still eyeing Nitrah and called out, "Yeah Tim, what's up?"

"I got someone over here I want you to holler at."

I leaned down and kissed Nitrah's cheek and said, "See you inside."

Her eyes trailed from mine and focused behind me. She tilted her head to the right in a curious, borderline confused way and said, "Wow. This is going to be awkward as hell."

I turned around and looked into a face I hadn't seen in years. The main person I let go of because of Nitrah. My former best friend.

Nitrah smiled and began to walk over to him, "Hey Michael. And who is this handsome fellow on your arm?"

She was referencing a baby he was carrying. I eyed the child and then Michael, but stayed planted in my spot sliding my hands into my pockets. Tim eyed me and signaled with his head for me to walk over and say hello. I thought about it, but then decided not to. It had been years since I had talked to Michael. Today of all days he was here. Holding a child.

Nitrah passed me and walks up to him crying out ooo's and ahhh's. I grunted with slight annoyance, but decided to put my immaturity to the side and actually humanize myself in this situation. "Your son?" I asked.

He nodded and said he was a junior. I looked behind him and noticed a woman on a phone standing in the direction he walked from. "Your wife?" I asked curiously. I'm not going to lie. This man and I fell out because he wanted Nitrah and I was hoping he said the woman was his wife to ease my conscience. To know that they will never ever be together satisfied my own selfish reasons.

Nitrah looked at the woman and asked, "Is that Brittany?"

"Oh yeah, that's my fiancé. Not quite the wife, but we are working on it." Michael waved her over and she began to wobble over. And I do mean wobble because she was pregnant again.

"Wow you guys are pushing these kids on out then." Nitrah walked over to Brittany and hugged her. Once she was close enough, I reached out for her hand and introduced myself.

Brittany smiled and said, "Oh, you're his old friend from college. Wow nice to finally put a face to the name." I smiled slightly, but looked at Michael confused.

Michael nodded his head yes, "I talk about you. I tell her some of the antics we use to pull. Yo Tim what's up? Where's Robert?"

I didn't have much time to digest that fact that a friend I abandoned a decade ago talks to his future wife about me. I wondered why but decided to answer his question instead, "Robert is inside. The service is about to being anyway. I'll take you all in." I turned to Nitrah and told her we would continue our conversation later. She waved me off. But I was indeed going to finish what I started.

Chapter 46

Nitrah

After Troy walked away I turned on my heels to see Dahlia standing behind the funeral home leaned up against the cement wall. I trotted over to her curious as to why she was hiding in the back. "Dahlia, why are you back here?" I asked. It seemed like the most logical question to ask. I knew she wasn't ok. We were about to bury our former best friend.

Upon hearing my voice Dahlia looked over to me and gave me a weak smile. "I just need a moment."

I planted my hand on her shoulder, something that felt totally weird as soon as I did it and rubbed it. "It's almost over."

A long two minutes passed before Dahlia managed to look at me again and state, "I left this city long ago to rid myself of the past. I had done some dirt. I had cried all I could cry and I wanted to forget. I had forged a stronger bond with Charmaine long after I left simply because I had crushed my other friends. But for the life of me I could never figure out why Charmaine initially sought me out to do her dirty work."

Tears streamed down Dahlia's face as she began her rant. My eyes widened with agony and confusion, but I kept my stance and my hand planted on her shoulder and listened. Out of the corner of my eye I noticed Jazz walking towards us. I formed my mouth in an O and told her to be quiet as she neared us. I didn't want to interrupt whatever it is Dahlia felt she needed to cry about.

"What do you mean?" I now had my hand mounted on the top of her back in a soothing motion. I leaned my body closer to hers to offer it as a place of temporary shelter to lean on. Jazz tiptoed closer to us, but didn't pass the corner where Dahlia could see her. I turned my attention back to Dahlia.

"I'm sorry Nitrah for everything that I put you through really. In college when I asked you to play that scam on Troy it was all..."

"All what?"

"I don't know any more. I used to play this over and over in my head, but now it's just doesn't make sense to me anymore."

"Well let me help you make sense of it all."

Dahlia leaned backwards away from me and took her hands and rubbed them across her face. She wiped away at her eyes and blew out hot air letting out a deep breath in the process. "I have wanted to tell you and Jazz for years, but I guess it doesn't matter anymore. Charmaine isn't here anymore." Tears dropped from her eyes as she said Charmaine wasn't here anymore. The irony of it all was that even though the statement was true, I was more focused on what the hell Dahlia was struggling to tell me. Should I blurt out let it out or should I be patient and hope she hurries this up?

"In college Charmaine and I were really close. Kind of how we were a year ago before she up and disappeared on me. But I remember the day like it was yesterday…"

ðˆˆ

Inside of our favorite café in downtown Chicago I noticed Charmaine mapping out a story plot. She was so stuck on writing this novel she had in her head that she had been nose deep in this journal for weeks now. I had met up with her during my lunch break to chat it up. It was a cold April day and I didn't want to travel far from my job on the 15th floor of the Stewart Plaza.

"You figure out the main characters name yet?" I asked.

Charmaine looked up from her journal and over to me across the table, "Girl I am so busy in this book that I am going to be the next Francis Ray! Just watch and see."

"Who?"

Charmaine rolled her eyes and laughed, "Only one of the most successful romance writers in African American fiction. Umm hello, you better catch up with the news honey child."

I laughed and waved her off, "So the name?"

"Nothing better than Timothy."

I raised an eyebrow and eyed Charmaine, "Char are you writing a book based on Tim, Jazz's ex-husband and your secret boo thang?"

170

"Well yeah, why not? He has given me plenty of material to write about. Him and his sorry ass."

"He may be sorry but, the brother is fine as hell."

Charmaine paused and then took a huge swallow of her latte. She squirmed in her seat and then rolled her eyes once more. I laughed and asked her why was she doing all of this eye rolling.

"You ever think about the scam we did in college?"

"Yeah."

"You know how I asked you to get Nitrah to date Troy and to dump him and yada yada so that you can get your revenge on him?"

"Yes Charmaine I remember damn. Broadcast all of my business to the whole place why don't you."

"I didn't tell you this though."

I tilted my head in confusion and dropped my fork in my plate. "Tell me what?"

"I was asked to come up with a plan for another bigger reason."

I sat there totally confused as to what my friend was trying to tell me. This was something that happened many years ago. It couldn't have been that deep of a secret because no way would she keep something like this from me for years. I played with my thoughts over and over in my head in an effort not to go off. I calmly said, "Keep going."

"We had just met Jazzaray and once Tim saw her he asked me to help him get her. I had done this before for him with plenty of other women. I was Tim's puppet for years. I know this now and I own up to it. But I am not anymore."

171

"Wait a minute. Hold up. Back up and rewind. Tim wanted you to do what?"

Charmaine looked away from me for a few seconds and spoke the words, "The scam was not to get back at Troy. It was to get us into Tim's circle. To get Jazz into his reach. He sought her from day one."

My mouth dropped in shock, "What? Huh? Wait what?" I noticed a couple seated next to us jump at the sound of my voice so I decided to lower my tone.

"I'm sorry."

"Wait a minute, so you were not the initiator. This whole time Tim was pursuing Jazz, used all of us to get there, married her, impregnated her, and all at the same time he was still fucking you?"

"Girl Tim always had women on the side. The man is psycho if you ask me. And arrogant as hell."

"How did you allow this man to manipulate you like this and then take the fall for everything?"

"He and Jazz have a child together. There was no need for me to cause any more headaches. So I took the blame and called it a day."

I pushed myself back from the table and just stared at her. I couldn't believe what I was hearing so I began to replay those events from the past in my head. But it was years ago, we were tipping on ten years later. I began to shake my head in disappointment. "You kept this to yourself?"

"Monica knows. This is why she helped me break up Jazz and Tim by sleeping with him."

"Y'all birth a different type of breed in North Carolina huh? Monica and you are on some other type of shit to play with folks lives like that. And I sat up here and did the same thing you did. I allowed you to use me as a pawn for your own selfish reasons. I allowed Nitrah and Jazz to think that I thought this whole shit up and for what? Not only do I not have them in my life anymore, but I lost a good guy in the process, Robert."

Charmaine chuckled and said, "Girl you lost Robert because you were jealous of Troy and Nitrah. You wanted Troy back by any means necessary. You see, you and I are more alike than you want to admit. How the hell do you think we ended up following each other to Chicago?"

"I thought it was because we were more than friends Char. We are family you know."

"Well I figured I would tell you anyways. Since I don't know how long I will be here in Chicago."

I rolled my eyes and said, "This Keith guy in DC again? Like are you serious Char? He can move here, not the other way around."

"I am finally over Tim and I got a guy who wants to try it out with me. I am going to take his offer."

I folded my arms across my chest and said, "You had a good guy. His name was Bobby. You married him remember."

"And he was fucking your sister Dahlia."

"That's after you pushed him away Char, damn. Own up to your own shit and don't throw my sisters actions in my face. I know what she is capable of. She got pregnant by my boyfriend remember."

Charmaine took another sip of her latte and pulled out cash from her purse. "Time to go."

I pushed back my seat and dropped cash on the table as well, "I totally agree."

ðð

I looked Nitrah in the face and noticed that her body wasn't leaned towards me any longer. Her hand wasn't planted on my shoulder and her eyes were pierced with darkness and anger. I took a couple steps backwards just in case this situation turned violent and suddenly saw Jazz walk around the corner.

I looked at Jazz who had already begun crying and I felt sorry. I felt more than sorry. I felt bad because I knew that she had to be in pain right now. I was in pain when I found out. It's not like I put Tim onto her, Charmaine did. But how do you get mad at a dead woman?

"I'm sorry," I managed to whisper.

Jazz walk up towards me and shook her head in disgust. "You got some nerve knowing about this and not saying anything."

In my defense I yelled, "I found out what a year ago and you two weren't in my lives any longer so what was the point?"

"This shit is sickening. This has to be a joke," Nitrah added.

"But you knew Charmaine developed the scam all those years ago. This whole time we thought you

174

masterminded this whole thing. What are you going to tell me now that Maxwell isn't genuine either?" Jazz was nearly shaking in anger. I walked over to her and placed my hand on her shoulder. I gave it a tight squeeze.

"No, Maxwell loves you. I know that when I see him look at you. This was all on me and Charmaine. We are just not as loyal as you and Nitrah have been to each other and I am sorry."

Jazz dropped her head into her hands as Nitrah rushed over to hold her. She angrily moved my hand so I took a few steps backwards to allow them to console each other. In that moment I knew I had no one who could console me. Monica was a friend, but she wasn't Nitrah or Jazz. I couldn't trust her like I was able to trust them.

Leaning up against the cement wall, I heard a man walk up behind me and ask, "Is this the funeral for Charmaine Wright?"

We all turned our attention to the voice and as my eyes connected to his face my mouth dropped in shock. I heard Nitrah call out, "Bobby is that you?"

"Hey ladies, yes it's me."

Chapter 47

Jazz

I wiped away the tears from my eyes as we each took turns hugging Bobby, Charmaine's ex-husband. He had left her years ago and we hadn't heard about him or seen him since.

"Hi! How have you been?"

"Just good. You all look nice. I mean for this occasion you all look lovely. I just came to pay my respects to Charmaine. I was heartbroken once I found out about her murder. Any?"

We all shook our heads no. "It had actually been a year since Dahlia had seen her. Jazz and I personally disconnected with her years ago," Nitrah added.

I waved my hand and told him to follow me and said, "Come on y'all it's about that time anyway."

As we made our way towards the front of the funeral home I spotted Maxwell and walked over to him. "Max this is Bobby, Charmaine's ex-husband." They shook each other's hands as I asked him to show Bobby in.

Once they were out of sight I looked at Dahlia and Nitrah and said, "I don't know where we are going to go from here. But I do know that I am over the past. Yes, I am going to confront Tim about this mess. But what's done is done. I have a son from this. I have a life that I brought into this world when I was in love. No shame in that. No matter how conniving he was. I can only forgive him for that because he gave me a life that I love and take care of every day. But Dahlia, I don't know where we go from here. I mean it's been years and I am not the one to fake it until I make it. You haven't been here for me or Nitrah. And although the memories and life we use to share together is bittersweet the clock cannot be reversed. I love you and wish the best for you, but let's not force anything. For now let's just say good bye to our girl and see what happens."

I looked at Nitrah for reassurance. Nitrah opened her arms and offered up a group hug. Dahlia and I squeezed ourselves into her embrace wrapping our arms around each other. "I love you both as well. Let's just get through this day." With released each other, turned on our heels, and marched into the funeral home. The final moment had arrived.

Chapter 48

Nitrah

I had to admit the soft ivory color of her casket made it easier to be able to walk down the aisle to our seats that were ion the front row. My eyes searched and my heart dropped. The room was empty, there were maybe thirty people. I couldn't point out anyone who didn't look familiar though. We all knew each other but the fact that none of us were her blood didn't sit well with me. I smiled slightly at some of the people as we make our final steps to our seats.

My eyes searched for Cameron. He wasn't here. I blew out a nervous breath knowing that people would ask why. I sat down next to Jazz who sat down next to Maxwell. Dahlia walked a few more steps and sat down next to Monica who had her face hidden by the biggest and darkest shades you could have imagined.

It was only a matter of minutes before the silence that had taken over the room was interrupted by Pastor Giles. I look onward and tried to pay attention to his ten minute speech about a woman he didn't know. I grew even more agitated by the fact that he didn't know her.

I jumped to my feet with my emotions boiling over. I didn't look back, but I could feel everyone's eyes burning into the back of my head. I smoothed my hands over my dress and walked over to the Pastor and said, "I know you mean good, but I would like to speak about the woman I use to know."

He reluctantly moved to the left of me after he surveyed the room for any objections. There were none. I waited for the right moment to speak. I was grateful that her casket was closed. I placed my hand on the top of it and eyed the pink roses that lay across it.

"I have known this woman since college. She was the closest person to me at one point in my life. If she asked me to climb a mountain to save her life I would do it. When I heard that Charmaine had died I felt a lot of guilt. I know that how we ended was bad, but now I can't help but wonder if it was worth it. What was the last thing I said to her? Could we get it right at this moment if she was even here? I keep replaying those questions in my head and for once in my life I can't change what has happened. They say we all hold fate in our hands, but this is the end. How do we come back from this?"

I fell silent as I fought back the intense pain that felt like a baseball stuck in the middle of my throat. I turned to face Charmaine's casket. Placing my hands on top of it I drop my head down and begin to cry out. I would had never imagined that one of us would die so young.

I felt the touch of someone's hand on my back and then another on my shoulder. I glanced to each side and see

Dahlia and Jazz, then Monica, then Troy. And one by one everyone began to make their way to us. Everyone was now gathered at Charmaine's casket with their heads bowed. The Pastor began to speak over the soft sobs as we had our final moments with her.

With each breath I took I gained a little more strength. One of the ushers at the funeral home came out and began to move the followers from her casket. Another one came out and motioned for me to move backwards. I did and everyone moved back as did I. I heard the clicks and creaks of the casket as they began to open the top. I felt the air leave my lungs as I gripped Troy's hand who somehow found himself standing right next to me.

I felt like the moment was in slow motion. I noticed everything. From the rise and fall of my chest to the way the silk bedding fell to the side as the casket top opened wider and wider and then I saw the tip of Charmaine's nose. I began to weep as more of her face was revealed.

The usher called out, "It's now time to say your final goodbyes." My eyes looked to the right of me as I noticed Tim make his way to the front. My tears felt like fiery acid was seeping through them as I tried to clear my vision to watch him. In a matter of seconds his body fell across the casket as he cried out. I had never seen him this emotional. Not even over Jazz. I eyed Jazz who now had dropped her face in her hands and was crying out. Maxwell took her into his arms and squeezed her tightly.

Dahlia and Monica walked up to Tim each taking on one of his shoulders and embracing him. I turned to Troy and laid my head on his shoulder. Wrapping his arms around me he whispers, "I love you."

I whisper, "I love you too."

ð ð ð

I walked into my room in Mama's house and kicked off my shoes. As I marched towards the bathroom the door swings open and Cameron walked out. "Cam hey!"

"Nitrah!"

"I thought you would be halfway to Houston by now."

"I slept in, packing now. I'll be out of your way in less than an hour." He tried to walk around me, but I grabbed his arm and gripped it hard.

"I buried my best friend today. Someone I use to love. Don't you get that?"

He snatches his arm away and says, "I buried something too. This relationship. I am no longer going to do the back and forth with you Nitrah. I am tired of you and Troy pretending that you all don't want anything from each other. All the while me and Gabrielle are being dragged along for the ride."

"So you're going to leave me?"

"I am letting you go Nitrah. I want to be happy. I want to be complete. I want someone who wants me just as much as I want them. And for once I realize that isn't you. You want him."

He marched over to the bed and drops a pair of shoes in his luggage and zips it up. "Give me a couple of days to be moved out of our home. I will talk to the kids."

I blurted out, "We will talk to the kids." He stared at me. I stared back. No doubt that I loved this man. But you can't help who you love more. He was right. This was it and he and I needed to call it quits while we still could. He walked up to me and stared into my eyes. I stared back challenging what it was that he saw in me.

"I love you," I managed to say.

"I love you too." Cameron said bending down and kissing me softly on the lips. With that he turned on his heels and grabbed his bag. In a swift move he walked out of the room. I heard the front door open and close and I fell down to my knees and cried.

"Even I saw this one coming." I heard Denim say as he strolled into my room.

"Don't start with me right now Denim. I don't need the drama or the extra." He walked past me and into the bathroom. He walked out with a roll of tissue and handed it to me. He grabbed me by my shoulders and lifted me onto the bed.

"So he left?" I nodded my head yes. "For good?" I nodded my head yes again. Denim kissed my forehead and began to rub my back.

"I don't need a speech ok Denim." I said with as much attitude as I could possibly muster up.

He laughed and said, "Girl I have known you since grade school. We were friends, then lovers, then friends again, and now family. I love you. I want you to be happy."

"And?"

"And I know that Nigga Troy is who you want. So stop wasting time."

I exhaled and didn't say a word for maybe three minutes before I replied, "I do."

"Yep we all know. Including that nigga. Just let me know when the wedding and shit is. I got you." He laughed and kissed my forehead again. "I hate to leave you like this but I have to catch a plane. Headed overseas in a few days."

"I'm going to miss you." I buried my head into his chest and wrapped my arms around him. He squeezed me back. We stayed in each other's arms from what seemed like forever before he got up to leave again. I knew it would be months before my eyes landed on him again. That is what made me sad. Ironically, I missed him more than I missed Cameron.

Desiring to get out of this funeral dress to meet everyone at Rhapsody later I got up off the bed and let my feet sink into the wool carpet when I heard someone say, "Are you alone?"

I looked at the front door of my bedroom and smiled, "Yes Troy, come on in."

Chapter 49

Troy

I closed the door and walked over to Nitrah, who was seated on the. I stood in front of her as she sat at the edge and began to run my fingers through her hair. Stooping downward I kissed her forehead, then her nose, and lastly I took my time and kissed her lips.

"I love you," I whispered. She grabbed my neck and pulled me down on top of her as our mouths hungrily tasted each other. I ran my hands aggressively over her body squeezing and hugging each of her curves. I wanted to remember her body next to mine just like the first time.

I moaned out as our efforts to pull each other out of our clothing became more of a battle. And it was a battle. I wanted this woman to know that in spite of my mistakes, in spite of my flaws, in spite of my marrying someone else to escape the pain, she was the one. I wanted her so badly that the past ten years began to race through my mind like a bad movie.

I could feel my emotions making its way through the tears that were forming in my eyes as the moment I was sharing with Nitrah was beginning to sink in. I pulled away from her with all the power that I could manage and asked, "No more back and forth?"

I searched her eyes to find any doubt as I waited for the response that I needed. She nodded her head yes and said, "I think it's time we did it differently. Don't you think?"

I pushed my forehead into hers never taking my eyes away from her and smiled. I loved this woman and in spite of her mistakes, my lies, the games, the drama, the continuous efforts to move on. This wasn't going anywhere. I wanted her badly and I wanted her now.

I guided my hand down her legs and planted them between her thighs. I felt her juices drizzle down my hand and as I had wanted since the very last time we were together our bodies were entangled into each other once again. This time I knew it would be the beginning to the rest of our lives together. After a day like this and realizing life was too short to play the merry-go-round game I decided to tell the woman I loved that I only wanted her. Finally, I was going to do it the right way.

Chapter 50

Jazzaray

I scooted into the booth and asked my server for a glass of water. Tim asked for an orange juice. It was early in the morning. One week after Charmaine's funeral. I had rested long enough before I could find myself back in front of Tim again. Dahlia was long gone back to Chicago but we promised to make an effort to stay in touch.

I took a deep breath and looked Tim over. He looked like shit. I scrunched my nose in disgust and asked, "Why do you look like this?"

"Been in hiding. Haven't done much of anything."

"So you needed to meet Tim. What's up?"

"I have been speaking to Michael since the funeral. He has some business opportunities out in Cali for me. I figure I need a change of scenery and to get away from Fort Worth."

I raised an eyebrow with a little curiosity but excitement at the same time, "As in move away? You consider Tim Jr.?"

"I am no good for him if I stay here. I am not happy Jazz. You moved on a long time ago. You have this family with ole dude and I have nothing. Even Charmaine has been gone out of my life for a long time now and now look. I need to do this for me."

I thought about his speech. I even saw the pain in his eyes. Something in me still wanted to call him out on the bullshit he pulled over a decade ago. Tricking and pursuing me. But then I thought why bring it up now with him leaving. This could be the chance I get to be Tim free. I could be without the drama, the exploits; Tim Jr. wouldn't have to be around all of his Dad's women. I could just be happy with Maxwell.

I thought of my long term happiness and decided on the latter, "This will make you happy?"

He shook his head yes. I gave him a weak smile and replied, "I want you to be happy and if this is it. Go for it." He reached over and grabbed my hand and squeezed it. As much as I wanted to pull away I didn't. I played the role of being that concerned ex-wife in hopes that he would in fact leave.

Two weeks later he did. It didn't affect Jr. as much as I thought it would seeing as though Maxwell had been there for him every day of his life since he was in diapers. I refocused on my book store and family after Tim left. And surprisingly my girl Nitrah did too finally moving back to Fort Worth after Troy filed for divorce.

It may have taken a tragedy for all of us to get our shit together, but in the end we did the best we could do and corrected our wrongs. I wasn't worried about the past any longer. I came to terms with Charmaine's death and Tim's betrayal and decided to move on. Besides I was too focused on telling Maxwell that we were about to have an addition to the family. I was crossing my fingers to have another girl. Only time would tell though.

Chapter 51

Charmaine

If I had known what I knew now would I do it differently? I don't know. We all walk life alone. We were born alone and we will die alone. And I did. I had gotten caught up with a man who lied to me. His name was Keith. Once I got to DC he turned me out. I was one of many women that he controlled. He and his wife Nadine. She was sort of his wife I guess, not that she had his ring or anything. But she helped control me and the other girls.

I asked myself how I could get caught up in a city where no one knew me and where the only way to escape Keith and Nadine's wrath was to allow them to sell me. I numbed the pain with drugs. It helped me forget the things those men made me do. It also helped me forget that there were people who were looking for me and that loved me.

But I forgot about them.

I didn't know the man who killed me. He was some guy Keith had wanted me to satisfy. Keith doesn't even know I was murdered. He thinks I just ran away. In a sense I did. I escaped my past and my present through death.

My death wasn't in vain however. Just look at everyone I used to love and know. They finally got it right because they felt bad about what had happened to me. But don't you feel bad about me. My pain has finally stopped. I flew away into the sky never to be seen again. And soon enough my old friends will forget about me. They forget about the way I died and move on so that they can be happy. And I want them to be happy. After all playing with people's heart is the ultimate no-no. It's time we stopped playing.

Don't cry for me. Live for me.

Find Tamika
Twitter @TamikaNewhouse
Instagram @BossladyTamika
Facebook:
https://www.facebook.com/BossLadyTamikaNewhouse
Site www.TamikaNewhouse.com

Also in stores

(DELPHINE PUBLICATIONS PRESENTS)

Lovely

LIES

a novel

BY LASHANTA CHARLES

DELPHINE PUBLICATIONS Presents

Her Sweetest
REVENGE 2

A NOVEL BY
Saundra

WE ARE TEAM DELPHINE

Twitter/Instagram @DelphinePub